"I've earned everything I have,

and I don't need you playing the philanthropist to my little match girl! I'm not selling my lease back to you. I've got another year, and I'm staying. Now get out of here. This is my shop, and you're not welcome."

"Alicia, be reasonable," Connan pleaded.

"I'm perfectly reasonable. No Goliath is going to take my shop away from me. Now get out."

His gaze took in the bewitching tangle of her red curls, but he spoke calmly and with unshakable conviction. "I promise you, this is only the beginning."

Dear Reader,

Welcome to Silhouette. Experience the magic of the wonderful world where two people fall in love. Meet heroines who will make you cheer for their happiness, and heroes (be they the boy next door or a handsome, mysterious stranger) who will win your heart. Silhouette Romances reflect the magic of love—sweeping you away with books that will make you laugh and cry, heartwarming, poignant stories that will move you time and time again.

In the next few months, we're publishing romances by many of your all-time favorites, such as Diana Palmer, Brittany Young, Emilie Richards and Arlene James. Your response to these authors and other authors of Silhouette Romances has served as a touchstone for us, and we're pleased to bring you more books with Silhouette's distinctive medley of charm, wit and—above all—*romance*.

I hope you enjoy this book and the many stories to come. Experience the magic!

Sincerely,

Tara Hughes
Senior Editor
Silhouette Books

CATY LEAR
Pursued by Love

Published by Silhouette Books New York

America's Publisher of Contemporary Romance

SILHOUETTE BOOKS
300 E. 42nd St., New York, N.Y. 10017

Copyright © 1987 by Caty Lear

All rights reserved, including the right to reproduce
this book or portions thereof in any form whatsoever.
For information address Silhouette Books,
300 E. 42nd St., New York, N.Y. 10017

ISBN: 0-373-08493-5

First Silhouette Books printing March 1987

All the characters in this book are fictitious. Any
resemblance to actual persons, living or dead, is
purely coincidental.

SILHOUETTE, SILHOUETTE ROMANCE and colophon
are registered trademarks of the publisher.

America's Publisher of Contemporary Romance

Printed in the U.S.A.

CATY LEAR

chose her pen name when she was ten years old, and had her first poem published when she was in the ninth grade. She published several poems in college, as well, but then got sidetracked for twelve years by an involving career in restaurant management. Now she's come full circle to her original love—writing—and finds it combines happily, if not smoothly, with the demands of family life and the antics of her two young children.

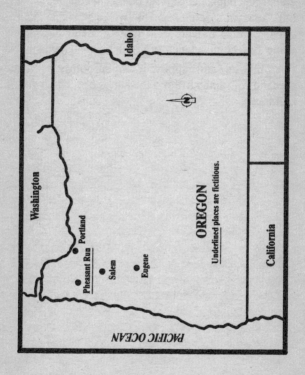

OREGON

Underlined places are fictitious.

Washington

Idaho

California

Portland

Pheasant Run

Salem

Eugene

PACIFIC OCEAN

Chapter One

Alicia covered the tiny table beside the door with a crisp blue-and-white-checked cloth. The classic color and pattern had become a trademark for the Panache Pantry, and she had reproduced it on all her labels. It was eye-catching on the cartons of tortellini salad, the jars of green pear chutney and all the other gourmet foods she produced in her shop. Her specialty products were becoming well-known in the Portland area, and one day she hoped her labels would be recognized throughout the state of Oregon.

She set plates with a blue-banded pattern at each place and oversized French jelly jars to use as water tumblers and then turned to the refrigerated display case to choose the delicacies most likely to impress the elusive, absentee landlord of Pheasant Run.

Cold tarragon-roasted chicken, she decided, and one of the more mildly seasoned pasta salads, just in case the Wraith had a delicate stomach. She smiled at

the nickname the retail tenants of Pheasant Run Château had bestowed on Connan O'Rourke when it became clear that he had no intention of concerning
himself with his new toy. They had all been intensely
curious about the new owner who turned out to be not
at all interested in them. Six months after his pur-
chase of the replica château and genuine winery, he
had yet to make an appearance. Even James Leandro, the manager, had only talked to him on the
phone.

Her green eyes narrowed as she carefully garnished
the plates with bunches of red and purple grapes. It
seemed odd that the ephemeral Wraith suddenly
wanted to deal directly with his small-time leaseholders. After all, the winery was a multimillion-dollar
business, and she would have thought that there were
more important things for the new owner to do. Of
course, she mused, he might just be bored with life on
the racquetball court and wanted to play lord of the
manor with his new château.

Under the old ownership, James Leandro had han-
dled all the day-to-day business details at Pheasant
Run. His relationship with the arcade tenants had been
highly visible and reassuring. Now, however, all that
was changed. James's duties had been redefined by the
arrogant new owner, and he was supposed to concentrate on marketing.

She had to fight down a rising tide of irritation at
the Wraith's sudden decision to handle all leasing decisions personally.

If she had been making the proposal to James today, she would have known exactly the right tack to
take. She would have emphasized her reliable record
and steadily increasing profitability and would have

modestly alluded to the glowing write-up Alicia Stevenson's Panache Pantry had received in the *Gourmet Review*. Dealing with the Wraith and his unknown prejudices mucked up everything, and God only knew what would impress him.

Sighing in frustration, she moved a small vase of bright yellow spider mums from the cash counter to the center of the table and stood back to gauge the effect.

"Very nice." A smooth, deep voice came from the doorway behind her, and Alicia turned with a startled smile on her lips. She'd been so engrossed in her thoughts that she hadn't heard anyone coming down the hall. The smile faded as she looked into the steel-gray eyes of the giant who stood there, and she felt an unreasonable sense of panic. He was easily six foot six, brown and hard-looking, a Goliath of controlled power and uncertain intentions. As he crossed the threshold to her side, every nerve clamored that she was being stalked, and she had to suppress an urge to retreat.

"I'm Connan O'Rourke." His eyes assessed her slightly flushed face. "Nice doesn't come close. I should have said perfect." His deep voice folded around her like rough velvet as he inventoried her barely five-foot-tall frame.

Alicia was stunned. There wasn't anything even remotely wraithlike about the confident, purposeful man who was lazily running his eyes over her. She was going to have to rethink her strategy fast. He didn't look like the mineral water type; old Burgundy seemed more his style. As for his digestion, it was probably case-hardened steel to match the rest of him. She stepped forward in a way that she hoped looked con-

fident and thrust out her hand to cover her confusion. "I'm Alicia Stevenson, Mr. O'Rourke. Welcome
to Pheasant Run, and thank you for seeing me today."

His oversized hand swallowed hers completely in a
firm handshake, and she swore that she could see little fires dancing in his eyes as they gazed down at her.
The man was huge, and she had to tip her head back
at an uncomfortable angle to meet his steady inspection. Defiantly she lifted her chin another inch and
then realized that she had ruined the effect by unconsciously backing away from him.

"Of course. We have business to discuss." For some
reason, his words sounded like a threat, and she
scrambled mentally to put a name to the intense reaction he inspired in her. Irritation, fear, distrust? She
had always disliked overly tall men. Not only did they
draw attention to her own lack of inches, but they
tended to be domineering and pushy when dealing
with lesser mortals. She was feeling very much the
lesser at the moment. She felt surrounded by him, and
she was angry at herself for the weakness.

"That's right," she responded, trying to keep the
belligerence out of her voice. "I'm interested in ex-
panding into the card shop's space when they vacate.
I want to increase my product line and add seating."
Alicia tried to read the chiseled brown face, but his
expression didn't give any clues to his thoughts. She
cleared her throat nervously and ran the tip of her
tongue over suddenly dry lips. "Do you have to go
somewhere?" she blurted out, motioning vaguely at
his standing figure. His presence was definitely getting on her nerves. When he shook his head, she added
coolly, "Please sit down. Lunch is all ready."

She tensed as he brushed by her to sit at the small table, and her skin tingled uncomfortably. He looked very relaxed as he sat down, returning an easy smile, and Alicia had the suspicion that he was amused.

"You've worked miracles with this tiny space," he remarked as he surveyed the arrangement of shelves and displays.

"Thank you. It's small, but up till now it's worked for me. As you can see, there isn't any real seating available here, so I've concentrated on developing cold gourmet picnic food. Of course, some of it reheats deliciously, like these tarragon hens, but most of the items are consumed as is on the grounds of Pheasant Run." Alicia paused. She knew that she was prattling. O'Rourke was giving her his full attention, but his expression was about as encouraging as a granite wall. "Go ahead. You can sample some of our specialties while I fill you in on my background here at the Pantry and the plans I have for expansion."

He picked up his knife and fork and sliced into the perfectly roasted bird. She watched as he brought a morsel to his mouth and slowly savored the redolent flavors of fresh garlic and tarragon.

His lips were firm and classically modeled. Their silky looking texture contrasted appealingly with the shadow of a beard along his jaw. Alicia wondered idly if he had to shave twice a day... wondered if his chest was equally... She braked the intimate progression of her thoughts and raised guilty eyes.

"If you don't stop looking at me that way, I'll skip the lunch and just have you for dessert," he said outrageously.

She started sputtering like Donald Duck. The man's gall was unbelievable. She finally managed to snap,

"I'm not on the menu," and retreated in confusion toward the kitchen, muttering about forgotten coffee.

Viciously buzzing coffee beans in the grinder, she cursed her wandering thoughts and O'Rourke's accurate reading of them. Not only was the brute unaccountably distracting, but he knew it and was enjoying every minute of her embarrassment. With a fierce gleam in her eye and a smile pasted on her lips, she marched in to face him.

He was leaning back in his chair and had stretched his mile-long legs out in front of him. For the first time in her life Alicia felt claustrophobic. The shop seemed full of him—shoulders, legs, and worst of all, those too-perceptive gray eyes that were gazing at her so enigmatically. She noticed that he had scarcely touched his food, and she had to swallow a remark about his needing to keep up his strength.

He looked at her quizzically. "Pax?" he asked.

"Pax," she agreed. The last thing she wanted was to engage in open hostilities with Connan O'Rourke.

He straightened in the small folding chair, and it creaked loudly beneath his weight. A harassed expression chased over his face, and Alicia felt a fleeting sympathy for his predicament. She knew how frustrating it could be outside the standard size range.

"Do you smoke?" she asked innocently.

"No. Why do you ask?" His expression was puzzled.

"I just wondered. They say it stunts your growth," she explained.

O'Rourke's chest heaved with barely contained laughter that finally overflowed and routed the last traces of Alicia's animosity. It was difficult to dislike a man who had such a captivating laugh. Suddenly he seemed human, accessible and very attractive.

"I think I'm over the worst of it," he said reassuringly. "I haven't grown an inch in the past six months. And don't worry about the chair—I think it's only buckled on one side."

Alicia had to laugh at his clowning as he inspected the lightweight chair with mock concern, and she couldn't resist responding in kind.

"It must be a terrible inconvenience—traveling in the cargo compartment and being banned from the balcony at the opera." Sympathy dripped from her words.

"At last, a woman who understands," he said theatrically "'Come live with me and be my love.'"

Alicia darted a quick look at his face and decided that she didn't like what she saw there. His words had been teasing, but the steely glint in those gray eyes had nothing to do with humor. They were uncomfortably determined looking. Uneasily she looked away, feeling like a sparrow under the piercing gaze of a hungry hawk. She regretted having let the conversation wander so far from business matters.

"What's wrong, Alicia?" he drawled. "Cat got your tongue?" For the second time he glanced over her small, graceful body. "That would be a pity. As far as I can tell, everything else is in superb working order."

Alicia remained speechless as the color flamed in her cheeks. O'Rourke wanted to make her aware of him and had succeeded. His deep voice was no less caressing than the expression in his eyes, and her body tingled from the effect. She fought to find her voice, fought to find a response that would put him firmly in his place. The last thing she needed was to have to fend off the practiced advances of an obvious womanizer.

"Of course a more detailed inspection might be fun even if it isn't strictly necessary," he continued devilishly.

Alicia's eyes narrowed dangerously. Her temper was close to a full-scale eruption. O'Rourke was the embodiment of everything she disliked in a man. He was big, domineering and expected women to fall into his arms out of sheer gratitude for his lordly attention.

"My balance sheets are the only thing you'll be inspecting around here, Mr. O'Rourke," she snapped at him.

She stalked around the table to sit in the chair opposite him. Somehow she felt more confident with the table solidly between them.

O'Rourke surveyed her through coolly assessing eyes and wondered what she was thinking. He knew he was rushing her, but there was something about the tiny redheaded woman that had set an unaccountable urgency ticking away inside him. He noted her heightened color with satisfaction. She was obviously aware of the volatility between them but was stubbornly refusing to respond to it. Then he measured her withdrawn expression and realized that it was tinged with bitterness. The idea shocked him. In the past women had responded to him in many ways, but never with loathing. He found the idea vaguely alarming. The lack of his usual finesse must have disgusted her. Well, he could force himself to slow down, but he wasn't going to stop. Alicia Stevenson intrigued and attracted him.

"Would you like some coffee?" Alicia managed to ask in a tight, frozen voice.

"Thanks. I could use some," he said sardonically.

"Do you use cream and sugar?" she asked politely, keeping her eyes on the thermos.

"No, just a cup will do."

Her eyes flew up to meet his laughing ones and then down to the table in dismay. She had forgotten the cups, and the wretch was positively enjoying her discomfort. She stood up and began to clear the table. "I'll get these things out of the way and bring back the mugs with my proposal," she retorted.

"By all means hurry back," he said with a grin. "I've never gotten a proposal before. Propositions maybe, but never an outright proposal."

She glared at him before turning sharply and stalking back into the kitchen. The man was impossible, she thought furiously. He seemed determined to avoid their business discussion. Well, he'd better resign himself to the facts of life. She wasn't interested in playing games with him; all she wanted was an extra 1,500 square feet of space. Like it or not, he was going to listen to her ideas. After all, he was the one who wanted to handle arcade leases. She hooked her fingers through the handles of two large mugs and grabbed a plate of assorted chocolate truffles from the refrigerator, then headed back into the arena with the light of battle in her eye.

Connan watched as she came toward him, the momentary vulnerability gone, her green eyes and auburn hair almost crackling with sparks. An attractive flush rode high on her cheekbones, and she looked ready to take on the world. At that moment he wanted to focus her fiery intensity on himself, wanted to feel her burning for him alone. He allowed himself to visualize the entrancing image of her surrender before he pulled himself back to reality. She was obviously going to need a lot of convincing.

Alicia thumped the mugs down and filled them, pushing one toward him with a casual gesture. She offered him the plate of truffles. "Cognac, amaretto and Grand Marnier," she pointed out succinctly. Settling herself comfortably in her chair, she took a swallow of coffee, closing her eyes for only a moment to enjoy the hot brew and to focus her mind fully for the coming encounter. She set down her mug and reached for the folder that lay on the table between them.

"Over the past year, my sales here have almost doubled. That doesn't include any of the outside catering we've done—that's a separate business." Alicia looked across the table to meet his eyes and almost faltered. The warmth and playfulness was gone, and a forbidding expression drew his eyebrows together above stern gray eyes. He didn't seem impressed with her information.

"In order to maintain this level of growth, I need more space. Then I can carry more products. I'm particularly interested in regionally produced foods— gourmet honey, local cheese, there's some really fine smoked seafood available, and specialty oils and vinegars. But most of all I need to increase the seating capacity inside. We need to be able to offer an alternative on rainy days. In the winter it's imperative if we are ever going to build any off-season traffic."

O'Rourke shifted uneasily in his chair as Alicia paused to draw a deep breath. God, she was beautiful, and dead serious about her expansion project. James Leandro had warned him that Alicia would be difficult to handle and would probably resist his plans for the arcade. Half an hour ago, Connan had been confident of his persuasive abilities, but now he found himself tempted to toss out all the expensive marketing surveys and give her what she wanted.

But that was impossible, of course. He knew he was right, and he would just have to salvage the situation as best he could. He could almost feel the noose he was tying around his own neck, but it was better to clear the air now rather than run the risk of being accused of deception later. He cleared his throat and tried to speak gently, but his voice came out abruptly, sounding harsh to his own ears.

"Alicia, I can tell that you've thought this proposal through, and under normal circumstances I'd hear you out, but you may as well save your breath. I've decided not to renew any of the arcade leases. I'm going to phase out the arcade shops and get Pheasant Run back into the serious business of producing the best wine possible. This hodgepodge of jewelry shops and knitting boutiques is totally out of place. Both the winery and the retail businesses will be better off when they part ways."

She looked into his eyes disbelievingly. She couldn't have heard him correctly. The winery's arcade hadn't come close to realizing its potential as a profit center. He couldn't be planning to dump the entire project.

"You mean that you're looking for new businesses that will be more in tune with Pheasant Run as a winery?" Asking the question gave her new hope. She'd had some second thoughts herself about the suitability of some of the tenants. Of course he'd want to reorganize the businesses.

"No, I'm sorry. There won't be any arcade when all the current leases expire. In fact, I'd like to expedite the process by offering to buy out the present tenants. I'd be more than fair. I'd give you enough to relocate and equip a larger shop in a better location.'' He was speaking too fast and knew that he sounded like a used car salesman.

For a stunned moment Alicia was silent, letting the sense of his words sink in. Then she realized what he was offering, and all the banked fires, all the thwarted enthusiasm, exploded out of control.

''You're not giving me anything! I've earned every thing I have, and I don't need you playing the philanthropist to my little match girl. I'm *not* selling my lease back to you. I've got another year and I'm staying. Now get out of here. This is my shop, and you're not welcome.''

''Alicia, be reasonable.''

''I'm perfectly reasonable. I've got a lot invested in the shop, and no Goliath is going to take it away from me. Now get out. I've got some serious business to take care of.'' She was almost shouting at him as fury and bitterness filled her. He'd been toying with her, softening her up before the ax fell.

He cursed softly, tension etched deeply on his face. His gaze took in the bewitching tangle of her red curls, but he spoke quite calmly and with an unshakable conviction. ''I promise you, this is only the beginning.'' With a last intent look at her flushed face, he turned and left as quietly as he'd arrived.

Alicia walked numbly back to the kitchen and stared at the well-organized space. The big bully had pulled her world down around her ears and sauntered away, leaving her standing in the rubble. The possibility of the arcade being shut down had never occurred to her, and she was stunned at the thought. She'd made the

Pantry her whole world, and now that world would no longer exist. Damn the man's arrogance, she thought furiously.

She slowed her angry pacing in a conscious effort to bring her temper under control. Pitching a fit wasn't going to solve her problem. She needed to analyze the situation and organize her options, then she could work on a plan of action. "I'll be damned before I'll roll over and play dead to suit Connan O'Rourke's convenience," she muttered to herself.

She slammed the front door and locked it, thankful that the arcade was closed on Mondays and that she wouldn't have to deal with any customers. She went to her desk and took a pen and a yellow pad and began to jot ideas down. The easiest thing to do would be to meekly accept O'Rourke's edict, take his buy-out money and relocate. It was also the least appealing idea.

She'd never been a quitter, and the thought of him getting his way so painlessly rankled. She could try to wait him out. There was almost a year left to run on her current lease, and anything could happen in that time. He might be run over by a train or hit by a meteor, she thought cheerfully, but she couldn't count on fate being on her side so magnanimously.

Well, she wasn't a quitter, and she couldn't picture herself passively hoping for miraculous deliverance from this villain's clutches. Her only other choice was to try some gentle persuasion to fight the unprincipled rat. After all, he hadn't even heard her proposal for arcade development. There was still a chance that she might be able to convince him that closing the arcade was premature, that it had potential as a moneymaker. She would have to call and make another appointment to see him.

Her pen slowed as her thoughts jumped ahead. How could she face him again? An hour ago she'd been screaming at him like a banshee. She stabbed her pen at the pad and cursed her temper. O'Rourke was probably working on an eviction notice right now. Alicia's defiance abruptly fizzled. No matter how much she detested the overbearing, overgrown creep, she should have controlled herself better. After all, on the purely legal level, he could do anything he wanted with his property.

On the ethical level, however, he had an obligation to both the leaseholders and the tourists who had come to depend on their services. She should have pointed all that out to him in a rational, businesslike way instead of behaving like a thwarted five-year-old. Her behavior had jeopardized not only the Panache Pantry but the other arcade shops as well.

Stuffing her notes into her briefcase gloomily, Alicia began to run through her mental checklist for closing—gas off, lights, walk-in locked. She grabbed her key ring from the hook over the desk and started for the front door when the phone rang. The harsh sound startled her into immobility, and she felt an icy foreboding slither down her spine. For the space of a heartbeat she considered ignoring the insistent summons, but then reminded herself that it was probably a customer and picked up the receiver.

"Hello, this is the Panache Pantry."

"Alicia! I'm glad I caught you...."

O'Rourke's deep voice was warm, and her body reacted as if it had been stroked. Her keys and briefcase slid out of her nerveless fingers and bounced off her knee. The sharp pain made her yelp and drop the phone. As she nursed her knee and scrambled in the tangle of cord on the floor, she muttered, "Damn you, Goliath."

He was chuckling when she got a grip on the phone again. "I like to have an impact when I call someone, but this has exceeded my wildest expectations. What happened? Did you throw the phone at the wall when you heard my voice?

Her knee was throbbing, and she had to bite back the words that were on the tip of her tongue. This was a reprieve, and she couldn't afford to throw it away. He was goading her on purpose, trying to get a reaction. She had no doubt that his technique with women was both sophisticated and effective, but he wasn't going to get a reaction from her—except frigid politeness.

"Nothing so theatrical I'm afraid. I tangled with the phone cord," she said indifferently. She held her breath for a moment before he spoke again. His voice had lost its velvet edge and started to sound a little ragged before settling into a more urbane mode.

"I see. I called to apologize about this afternoon. I was rather abrupt. Why don't you join me for a glass of wine upstairs before you leave for the day? It's the least I can do after that delicious lunch you provided for me."

Alicia was surprised at his apology. After all, she was the one who had lost her temper and done all the shouting. Still, she was being given a second chance to convince him that phasing out the arcade was a mistake, and that was an opportunity she couldn't pass up.

"That's very kind of you, Mr. O'Rourke. I'll be up in fifteen minutes."

"I'll be waiting," he said softly.

Alicia tried to shrug away the shiver that coursed down her spine. His slightly husky bass voice had the strangest effect on her. She almost felt like purring.

Abruptly she turned off that particular thought and went to brush her hair and put on fresh lipstick. "I'm doing this for my own self-confidence," she told her reflection defiantly.

After locking up the Pantry, Alicia climbed the broad marble stairs to O'Rourke's top-floor office suite. She tapped on the massive mahogany door, and it opened instantly.

O'Rourke smiled down at her, and she felt her own lips soften and smile in return. He took her arm with one large brown hand and ushered her past the deserted receptionist's desk and into his inner sanctum.

With its high ceiling and carved wainscoting, the room was magnificent, Alicia thought. But inexplicably it was O'Rourke her eyes followed.

She watched as he crossed the room to an alcove and pulled a long-necked bottle out of an ice bucket. He opened it with practiced ease, and she found herself smiling at his economical movements. O'Rourke obviously didn't believe in wasting time on unnecessary ceremony or flourishes.

Looking over his shoulder, he caught her smile and grinned back at her. There was no mistaking the satisfaction in his expression. She had seen that same look on Peter's face a hundred times.

Alicia's smile faded as she walked jerkily to the windows on the other side of the room. Damn, her guard had slipped for a moment, and O'Rourke was sure to take advantage of the fact. He was the kind of man who hammered the world into a shape that suited him. He would make no compromises and give no concessions. Like Peter, he would overwhelm and consume any woman who let herself get too close to him.

Her fingers clutched a heavy brocaded fold of drapery as she stared out the window. She had given up being a pale little shadow three years earlier, and nobody was going to get the chance to diminish her that way again.

"Why the frown, Alicia? Take a sip of this Riesling and relax."

O'Rourke had moved so silently across the room that she hadn't been aware of his presence close behind her until he pressed a crystal goblet into her hand and folded her fingers around the stem in an intimate gesture.

She turned to face him and tried to look at him objectively. He was shrewd and intelligent and was obviously used to command. His large muscular body moved with purpose, and his sense of humor was unexpected and a little devilish. All in all, he was a very compelling man—and a very dangerous one, she warned herself.

Alicia put a little more space between them and raised her glass. "Thank you. I think the Riesling is my favorite of all the wines produced here at Pheasant Run."

O'Rourke moved a little closer. "I really am sorry about this afternoon. I'm not known for my patience, but I should have been more sensitive to how you feel about the Panache Pantry. I'm glad you haven't written me off as a complete ogre."

Alicia gritted her teeth. He was standing so close that they were almost touching, and it was getting on her nerves.

"Not at all, Mr. O'Rourke. In fact, after my emotional reaction, I'm grateful that you've given me a second chance to explain my plans for expansion and promoting the arcade."

His silence stretched across the minutes, and Alicia held her breath, suddenly afraid that she had misconstrued his apology.

"Alicia." His voice was strangely gentle. "I'm looking forward to the pleasure of your company over a glass of wine, but this was purely a social invitation. I have no intention of discussing the issue of the arcade any further. My research was thorough and my decision is final."

Alicia put her glass of wine down on the windowsill with a snap and drew a deep, ragged breath. "In that case I won't waste any more of your time." She turned and walked toward the door, ignoring the surprised expression on O'Rourke's rugged features. After closing the door behind her, she scurried out of his offices and down the marble staircase.

As she got outside and walked across the parking lot, apprehension began to jostle her thoughts. In retrospect, every word that Connan O'Rourke uttered seemed to carry an implicit threat. What had been his parting shot when she threw him out of the Pantry after lunch? "I promise you, this is only the beginning," he'd said. The beginning of what? Had he uttered a declaration of war against the shop and its intemperate owner? If that was the case, why had he invited her for a glass of wine? Alicia wondered if she was being paranoid. The man inspired something very like panic in her, and she had to admit it was only partly related to his power over the future of the Pantry. There had been something in his expression, something in the gray depths of his eyes that had her almost trembling.

She shoved her hair away from her eyes with a hunted gesture and jerked open Mable's door. The ten-year-old van groaned a metallic protest, and Alicia patted the oxidized paint affectionately.

"Sorry, old girl. You're beginning to feel your age, aren't you?"

For once, Mable started like a pro, and soon she was driving off the château grounds and onto the narrow access road that led to Carlton. Shaking off the urge to replay every detail of her conversation with O'Rourke, she clamped a lid on her chaotic thoughts and resolved to enjoy the rest of the afternoon.

She stopped at a roadside produce stand and picked up a quart of unfiltered apple juice and a bag of pears and apples for an impromptu picnic in the red-and-gold autumn afternoon and headed Mable down the back roads that would eventually bring her back to Portland.

The sun was unseasonably warm as she drove through the fertile northwest corner of the Willamette Valley, through picture-book scenery rich with the harvest scent of ripe fruit and fallen leaves. The pastoral beauty inspired a mood of gentle introspection within Alicia. The recent pattern of her life had been one of incessant work and a single-minded attention to all the details of her business. She had consciously created a life-style that made soul-searching almost an impossibility. She'd chosen to live in the perpetual present tense, a door shut firmly against the

past, and the future only considered in relationship to
her work.

She could feel the tension ebbing as her taut body
unclenched, and she admitted for the first time that
she had been working too hard. The tourist season had
been a marathon, and even with the end of summer,
she hadn't allowed herself time to play. It had been
months since she had taken a day off with no dead-
lines or pressing business to attend to.

Every moment of her waking time had been spent
at the Pantry, and she recognized that the focus of her
life for the past three years had been extremely narrow. She had been hardly aware at all of the turning
of the seasons or the passage of time itself for that
matter. In some ways, the Panache Pantry was as
much a prison as a sanctuary. She brushed the disloyal thought aside and reminded herself that at the
age of twenty-four she was a confident and successful
businesswoman.

She caught the perfume of tree-ripened pears and
apples rising out of the paper bag beside her, and her
stomach knotted in response. It was way past her usual
lunchtime, and she was starving. She pulled off to the
side of the road and opened the jug of cider to take a
big swallow. Then she grabbed her picnic lunch and
ran down a shallow bank toward the faintly heard
sound of a stream.

The terrain was dappled with sunshine that filtered
through a golden canopy of birch and alder trees, and
the leaf-strewn ground sloped gradually down to the
stream she had heard from the road. The water was
clear and burbling, and she looked around for the
perfect vantage point and found it in a large weathered log that stuck out into the middle of the water.

She sat down on the mossy trunk and tipped her head back. The canopy of trees was not so thick here, and she was able to see patches of clear blue sky twinkling through the golden leaves. She savored the feel of the sun against her closed eyelids for a moment and then turned her attention to her picnic.

Taking large bites of apple, she let her thoughts flit pleasantly from one image to another, remembering places like this from another less complicated time in her life. The days would never have that childish simplicity again, she knew, but she could certainly try to bring more balance to her life and try to recapture some of her old intrepid attitude to the world.

It hardly seemed possible that the deli had absorbed three years of her life. O'Rourke's bombshell had one positive result, anyway. Her panic at the thought of losing Panache Pantry forced her to realize how dependent on it she had become. She knew that it wasn't any more healthy than her relationship with Peter had been and resolved to stop being so obsessive.

The shadows had lengthened, and a chill was beginning to tinge the air. She brushed herself off and made her way back to the waiting van. She hummed as she drove, feeling at peace with herself. Vague thoughts of O'Rourke nibbled at the fringe of her consciousness, but she was able to keep them at bay. The warm afternoon air flowed past in an uninterrupted stream as she made her way back to Portland and her small southside apartment, which had a view of the Willamette River.

She finally arrived at the entrance to the underground garage and parked in her usual space near the elevator. The concrete walls were chill and damp, and she could feel the glow of the afternoon fade as she waited for an elevator to take her to the third floor.

Chapter Two

Tuesday morning Alicia woke with the bewildering sensation that something was wrong. She had spent a restless night, dreaming she was pounding on the locked doors of the arcade and battling a whole army of dark giants. She narrowed her eyes against the sunlight that was pouring in through her bedroom window and realized that, due to her restless night, she'd overslept. She never bothered with an alarm clock because her internal clock was so reliable; summer and winter she woke promptly at six and had done so since she was a child.

She padded out to the kitchen to check the time and was dismayed to see that it was a quarter past seven. Frowning, she went through the ritual of making coffee. She hadn't overslept in years, not since those first months after Peter had left. She shied instinctively away from the dark memories and headed for the

bathroom. O'Rourke had cast his insufferable shadow
even into her dreams.

She took a hurried shower and dressed in her cus-
tomary button-down shirt and dark trousers. She
knotted a red knit tie under her collar and sipped a cup
of coffee as she quickly applied a little blusher and eye
shadow. Then, grabbing her briefcase, she ran down
four flights of stairs to the basement parking garage
and turned her van's rumpled nose toward the freeway.

Forty minutes later she pulled into the parking lot
behind the château and unclenched her fists from the
steering wheel. Freeway construction had snarled the
traffic, and Mable's controls had been designed for a
much larger person. She grimaced at her child-sized
hands and wished for the millionth time that she was
six inches taller. Her size was a constant source of
frustration that complicated even the most mundane
aspects of her daily life.

The Pantry's distinctive fragrance wrapped around
her as she opened the bright blue door and walked into
the orderly shop. Her assistant, Richard, was there
before her, and she could hear him on the kitchen
phone ordering produce. She waved at him as she entered the kitchen and set her briefcase down beside the
desk.

"Must have been some party," Richard murmured, giving her a faintly curious glance as he hung
up the phone. "You've never been a minute late in the
two years I've worked for you."

"I hate to disappoint you, but my life's not that exciting. I was overtired and overslept."

"Well, you missed the state visit."

Alicia looked at him inquiringly. Richard's sense of humor could be obscure.

"You know, the main man." Richard lowered his voice to a hoarse whisper. "The Wraith of Pheasant Run materialized on the doorstep at 7:35 this morning."

Alicia's heart lurched. "What did he want?"

"He said that he wanted you." Richard watched with interest as a wave of color washed over her ivory complexion. "That is, he said that he wanted to talk to you. Apparently he knew that you were always in by seven-thirty. I told him that you must have had a late night because you've never been late before."

"Did he say what he wanted to talk to me about?"

"No, he just turned and stomped off, looking big and mean. Definitely not a morning person I'd say."

Alicia felt something coiling in the pit of her stomach and struggled for a moment before responding with only the faintest show of interest. "How odd. He didn't leave a message, I take it."

"Not a word. How did your lunch meeting go, by the way? Martha said she saw you feeding him. Did you have enough food? A guy that size must eat a side of beef for breakfast, probably raw."

Alicia had to laugh as an image of the austere O'Rourke gnawing on a haunch of beef flashed through her mind. "I don't know. We didn't get around to eating."

"You didn't get around to eating? So what was the idea?"

Alicia looked at Richard with exasperation. He was insatiably curious about anything connected with the shop. In the past she'd always encouraged his involvement, but now she found herself reluctant to discuss the disastrous interview. She still hadn't come to terms with her feelings for Connan O'Rourke. She'd committed herself to fighting the arrogant landlord, but she knew that her weapons were pitifully inadequate. She desperately needed time to think and plan.

But why had he stopped by this morning? Why did he want to see her? Her mouth went dry as his rugged, massive form took shape in her mind, and she could hear the echo of his voice like the muted rumble of ocean waves. She shook her head and met Richard's assessing glance.

"I guess you could call it a difference of opinion, resulting in both of us losing our appetite," she said reluctantly.

"You mean you lost your temper?"

"You know me too well. Yes, I blew up, but I haven't given up. I'm still working on Phase Two of the campaign."

Richard seemed satisfied with her explanation and returned to his order sheet. "Do you want me to get some of Dick's hydroponic basil or should we order the frozen puree?"

"I suppose he wants a percentage of Fort Knox for it."

"Two fifty a bunch."

"Let's go for broke. I'd like to make that marinated mozzarella salad, and I can't use the frozen for that. But tell him that if the price goes any higher, we'll see him next spring."

"Aye, aye, Captain Bligh." Richard grinned at her, then asked, "By the way, have you got anything in mind for the bank shindig next week?"

She poured herself some coffee, thinking at the same time that she was drinking too much caffeine, and joined Richard at the desk.

"I thought we could do the stuffed mushroom caps and some of your fabulous canapes. Mary Alice Brannish has a new batch of goat cheese ready. We could use it on a cheese tray featuring all Northwest-made products."

"Sounds good. I've got a new canape I want to try. What do you think of chutney, cream cheese and curried prawns?"

"It sounds disgusting," she answered honestly.

"Well, maybe not the cream cheese. I'll fix some up and you can try it."

"I also want to use the local sturgeon roe instead of caviar. Do you think that you could track some down for me?"

"No problem. Now what about the display? We need a centerpiece to give some height to the table."

His question was put laconically enough, but Alicia knew he had been hoping to do an ice sculpture. "You'd better order a fifty-pound block of ice as well. An ice carving should give us all the height we need." She smiled at the almost beatific expression on his face. "Have you decided on a subject yet? I suppose you could always immortalize the retiring president's initials in ice."

Richard looked at her with a pained expression and assured her in lofty tones that he did neither initials nor dates. He was an *artist*. She handed him her notes and asked him to look over the rest of the proposed menu, make suggestions and then take care of the necessary ordering while she worked up a new batch of cognac truffles. He nodded agreeably as she put on the long white butcher's apron that fell to her ankles.

"What about the tasting upstairs tomorrow?"

She felt as if a trapdoor had opened beneath her feet and she was falling through a black void. How could she have forgotten? Her mind worked frantically as she tried to think of a way to avoid attending the affair. O'Rourke was sure to be there, and she knew that she couldn't face him this soon. She had to stay out of his way until she had a chance to organize her defenses more thoroughly. Richard was looking at her curiously, waiting for an answer.

"It slipped my mind," she admitted, "and I have another commitment." She looked at him searchingly for a minute before saying slowly, "You could stand in for me. It's not a big deal, mainly baby-sitting the table to make sure that the trays are full and that the table looks tidy."

"Not me. It's not my style at all. I like to be safely in the background, out of reach of all the PR slush you have to dish out."

"It would only be for a couple of hours. Richard, I wouldn't ask if there was any way I could be there myself." At least that part was the truth, and some of her very real desperation must have gotten through to him, for he nodded his sandy head in reluctant agreement.

"Okay, but you owe me for this one."

Relieved, she grinned and returned to the worktable, lining up the ingredients for her confections: unsalted butter, imported chocolate, sugar and the aged cognac that she preferred. She found it therapeutic working with her hands at a familiar task. She chopped the chocolate into small pieces and placed it over simmering water to melt while she creamed the butter and sugar together. Tasting and checking for volume, she was totally engrossed in her task and didn't hear the outer door open.

As she reached for the bottle of cognac to add to her mixture, she looked up to see O'Rourke standing in the doorway. He looked larger than ever and more dangerous. She couldn't do anything but stare at him and clutch the bottle to her.

He stood there silently, inspecting the pale skin of her cheeks, noting the veins that laced the fragile skin at her temples and the fevered brightness behind her eyes. His glance skimmed her figure, and she felt her body tingle as if he had touched her.

Richard was watching the frozen tableau with curiosity, and Alicia struggled to break the awful silence. She forced herself to move toward the table and set the bottle down as if it were the most priceless thing in the world, then turned to O'Rourke.

"What an honor, Mr. O'Rourke. We're rather busy right now, as you can see, but how can we help you?" She was proud of her self-control and the cool words she had tossed to him like a snowball. Richard was looking rather shocked at her cavalier treatment of the château's new owner, but as usual he kept his thoughts to himself.

"I have some business to discuss with you. Can you come up to the office for half an hour?"

She cursed the adrenaline that rushed through her body at the sound of his clipped voice and had to remind herself that she couldn't let him get to her. She couldn't afford to show any weakness, or he would be at her throat in a minute. He was still waiting for an answer, and she replied in an icy tone, "I'm afraid it's out of the question today. I'm right in the middle of something. If it's so important, we can talk here.''

Frustration appeared briefly on his face, but he didn't force the issue.

"If that's what you want. It's about tomorrow's tasting. We're hosting some buyers from the Midwest and I want to make sure everything goes smoothly. I haven't attended one of these functions before, so I wanted you to fill me in on your end of things so that I'd know what to expect.''

Alicia had to admire his control. She could certainly learn a few things from him. She made a strong effort to match his impersonal tone, as if the topic being discussed was one of total indifference to her.

"We keep it simple. The food is meant to complement the wine rather than the other way around. We've planned on sending up French bread, unsalted crackers, an assortment of hard and soft cheeses and a tray of fruit.''

She looked at Richard, busy making notes at the desk, and asked, "What were you able to come up with for fruit this time?''

He replied without looking up from his work, "Kiwi, New Zealand strawberries and blueberries, those Japanese pears you're so wild about, three kinds of local apples and maybe some decent melon, if we get lucky.''

Alicia picked up the cognac again and splashed a generous amount into the truffle mixture. Not meeting O'Rourke's eyes, she continued, "Richard will set up a table at five-thirty in the private tasting room and bring out the trays at a quarter to six. He'll keep an eye on things during the tasting and bring out backup trays of anything that runs out. Then he'll clean up after your guests leave.''

O'Rourke had been nodding in approval at the arrangements until she mentioned her assistant's attendance. His face darkened, and a muscle in his jaw began to jump. The bored facade dissolved to reveal the ruthless autocrat behind the mask.

"When I talked to James about it, he mentioned that you personally oversee these tastings. In fact, he looked on you as the unofficial hostess. This meeting is too important to me to jeopardize it by a last-minute change in format. I want you to take care of it in person.''

His voice was inflexible, and one glance at his face told her that his mind was made up. Well, her mind was made up, too. She wasn't going to do him any favors, and she wasn't interested in pandering to his already overinflated ego.

"Richard is perfectly competent to handle a few trays of cold food. Nothing could possibly go wrong. I have a prior commitment that evening and it's impossible for me to attend,'' she said in a voice that had dropped below the freezing point.

She looked at Richard for moral support and found him watching her with amusement.

"Standoff,'' he mouthed silently.

O'Rourke caught the silent interchange and scowled forbiddingly.

"It's not Richard's competence at issue. I'm sure he's very talented, but first impressions can be critical, and these people are used to dealing with only the principals in every field. I want the owner of the shop there, not the assistant. If you can't do it, I'll have to make other arrangements.''

Rage boiled within her. How dare he play so dirty? He knew the Pantry depended on catering the winery's tastings to help get through the slow season. What he was doing was no better than blackmail.

"In that case," she said through clenched teeth, "I'll just have to change my plans."

"Thank you." He grinned suddenly, unexpectedly, and for a moment the austere, autocratic face looked almost boyish. "I appreciate your cooperation," he added in a sincere-sounding voice. He took a step toward her and began to stretch out his hand. Alicia was startled by the gesture and instinctively backed away.

O'Rourke's face hardened into its more familiar harsh lines at her retreat, and his gray eyes narrowed thoughtfully as he looked at her.

That air of fine-boned fragility was deceptive, he thought critically. Her hair was pulled back from her face and twisted into a heavy knot that he found strangely fascinating. He imagined loosening the pins one by one and running his hands through the seductively curling mass. He could almost picture the bright strands drifting across the smooth skin of her shoulders. The thought smoldered in his mind, and he realized that he wanted her.

Abruptly he turned to the door. His sense of timing had never failed him so completely. Alicia Stevenson hated his guts, and there wasn't a damn thing he could do to change that fact. As he reached the door, he half turned and said wryly, "I'll see you tomorrow night then."

Her image stuck in his mind as he climbed the stairs to his office. That long white apron should have had a neutering effect on her figure, but instead it had accentuated her small, taut waist and the surprisingly voluptuous swell of her high breasts. His hands itched to trace the intriguing contours of her body, and he cursed himself impatiently. She was beginning to dominate his imagination.

Alicia was fuming. Her mind methodically considered ways to get even with the oversized, unprincipled rat.

"How about boiling oil?" Richard's voice came helpfully from the corner where he was beginning preparation of the promised prawn and chutney canapé.

"It's too fast. I was thinking of something much slower, like feeding him into the grape crusher inch by inch."

Richard laughed and returned to his chutney chopping. He cast one or two interested glances in her direction but didn't question her about her animosity toward O'Rourke. She covered the copper bowl and carried it to the walk-in to cool. The chocolate had to set so that she could shape it. She looked at her watch. It was nine o'clock, and the arcade would be open for business in an hour. She didn't expect many customers; maybe half a dozen would find their way to the winery during the course of the day, and only a few of them would buy anything from the Pantry.

She remembered last winter and how she'd nearly gone crazy with boredom, bouncing off the walls of the empty shop. That was when she had begun to develop her master plan for the expansion of the Panache Pantry. That was all wasted effort now that Connan O'Rourke had sabotaged any chance for growth.

She stood perfectly still in the middle of the room, arrested by the daring thought flitting along the fringes of her mind. Why not form a tenants' rights group and fight his plans to tear down the arcade? Even if they failed, it would stall things for a while and give people more time to plan for relocation. Best of all, it would make O'Rourke furious to have his high-handed plans interfered with. Her eyes flashed with enjoyment as she considered ways and means to thwart him.

"You look like the Cheshire cat. If you had a tail, you'd be lashing it right now. You know, I feel sorry for your Mr. O'Rourke. He won't know what hit him."

Alicia was startled at Richard's accurate reading of her mind. Was she so transparent, or was it just that she was predictable? Neither thought pleased her. "Don't waste your pity, and he's not my Mr. O'Rourke."

"Have it your way then," he said indifferently, but Alicia felt compelled to set him straight.

"You're way off base this time, Richard. He just has a power complex and is frustrated because I don't agree with everything he says. Look at the way he got nasty when I told him I couldn't come to his little wine tasting."

"I would have called it desperate, not nasty. Not only that, he was happy as a clam when you got mad at him after the Snow Queen routine. I'd say he's got the hots for you." Richard nodded emphatically at her.

Alicia felt suddenly cold as the unwelcome thought settled in her mind. It hadn't occurred to her, but O'Rourke would be just the type to use seduction as a weapon to get what he wanted. Something fragile crumbled inside her. She'd had enough of being used to last a lifetime. She looked at Richard's mischievous face and pulled herself together. "I hadn't noticed," she said coolly. "But if you're right, he can just go up in flames. I'm not in the fire-fighting business."

Richard threw up his hands in surrender. "Whatever you say, boss."

"How about watching the shop for me?" she asked. "I want to say hello to Martha."

He nodded agreeably. "Sure. I have it on good authority that I'm competent."

She walked the few steps to Martha's Knitting Boutique and tapped on the glass to get her friend's attention. The older woman turned from the handmade scarves she was arranging and looked up. With a big grin, she came to the door and opened it for Alicia. "I can hardly give those dratted things away. No one appreciates quality anymore."

"Nothing is going to sell if there aren't any buyers around," Alicia noted grimly.

Martha was looking at her speculatively, then nodded toward the back of the shop where two rocking chairs were positioned against the wall. "Let's sit down. It sounds like you have something on your mind."

Alicia followed her to the corner and settled herself in one of the chairs. "O'Rourke wants to phase out the arcade." She came right to the point.

Martha stared at her in astonishment. Her mouth hung open, and she closed it with an audible snap. "Is that what he told you yesterday?"

Alicia's laugh was short and unhumorous. "I certainly didn't make it up. He told me that he wanted to clear out the hodgepodge businesses in the arcade so that Pheasant Run could get down to the serious business of making wine." She laughed again, a short, bitter bark that grated painfully on the nerves. "Then he had the gall to offer to buy out the remaining time on my lease so that he could expedite closing the arcade."

Martha seemed to be struggling to find her voice. "What did you say to that?" she finally managed to ask.

"I won't go into all the gory details, but I don't think Mr. O'Rourke will try handing me a check anytime soon."

Martha nodded thoughtfully. "Somehow I didn't think you had accepted his offer."

"No, I didn't accept his offer. I'm going to fight him. I've worked too hard to establish the Pantry here to give it up on the whim of a giant, egotistical, insufferable, power-hungry profiteer.

"I take it you didn't like him much."

"Not much," Alicia agreed.

Martha gave her a long, considering look. "I know you've got your heart set on staying put in the arcade, but you know, Alicia, a new location might offer even more than what you've got here."

"You've got to be kidding. The arcade has everything I want. Besides, I don't like being pushed around, and I plan on getting a lot of satisfaction out of proving that point to the high and mighty O'Rourke."

Martha looked at her doubtfully. "I hope you're not biting off more than you can chew, Red."

"Save your worries for the Knitting Boutique, Martha. Now, do you want to hear my plan?"

Martha rubbed her gnarled hands together and nodded emphatically. "You bet I do. If you're really going to go after the giant, you can count on me."

Alicia smiled and leaned forward to press Martha's hand affectionately. "Thanks, Martha. Your support means a lot to me." She sat back in her rocker and set the chair into gentle motion. "Obviously, we can't accomplish too much by ourselves. O'Rourke is a mighty big fish and we're just a couple of tadpoles. So, the first thing we have to do is muster all the support we can. We've got to talk to the other tenants and let them know what's going on."

Alicia's reflective tone hardened, and she continued with quick, fierce determination. "Then I think we should try to organize a formal tenants' rights group and decide on a cooperative plan of action. Most of the tenants have a year or more left on their leases, and that's definitely a plus for us. I don't think O'Rourke can force anyone out without landing in a lot of hot water. I'll check on that with my lawyer. The important thing, though, is that we act as a group. That'll be our real strength. We don't want anyone succumbing to his buy-out offer if we can help it."

"You've given this problem a little thought, haven't you?" Martha's eyes twinkled with mischief.

"I haven't thought about anything else since Goliath informed me of his plans."

"Well, why don't you let me take care of the first part, the talking to folks. I gossip with everyone anyway, so it will be easy to stir up a little interest."

"Great. In the meantime, I'll be in contact with my lawyer and find out exactly what our legal position is."

"That's what I like about you, girl. You think big."

Alicia grinned at her and walked back to the Pantry with a distinctly jaunty step.

"If that smirk was any bigger, your face would fall off," Richard greeted her when she returned.

"This is not a smirk. This is a triumphant smile of supreme satisfaction."

"If O'Rourke had any sense at all, he'd head for the hills. He doesn't stand a chance with both you and Martha gunning for him. Thank God I'm not your target. I'd whimper and go paws up in a minute."

Alicia laughed at him. "Not you, Richard. You'd confuse us with your brilliant repartee and then you'd flatten us with one of your famous one-liners." She nodded at a stack of boxes by the door. "What came in?"

"One is from the asparagus people in California, one from Wild Berry Works and three from New York."

"That was fast. I didn't expect any of those shipments until next week. If you want to make up the fresh salads, I'll do the unpacking."

He nodded agreeably and ambled back into the kitchen. Alicia found a razor knife and went to work on the cartons. As she uncrated the jars of pickled asparagus and wild berry preserves that were destined for Christmas gift baskets, her sense of elation began to fade. O'Rourke would be a formidable opponent and, no doubt, a ruthless one as well.

He probably had a whole platoon of high-powered lawyers under his thumb who would delight in turning her into mincemeat. If she was going to go through with her hastily conceived campaign, she had to do it with her eyes open. It was risky, she had to admit. If she gambled and lost, O'Rourke would no doubt find a way to invalidate the remaining time on her lease and she'd lose everything. On the other hand, she reminded herself, if she didn't try she'd only have a year at best anyway.

Intellectually, she tried to face the possibility of being forced out of the arcade, but found it was impossible. Her emotions kept clouding the issue. The thought of being forced out inspired something very like panic in her. Pheasant Run and the arcade were an important part of what the Panache Pantry was, and it wouldn't be the same anyplace else. She knew the future might hold a forced relocation, but she couldn't bear to examine the fact very closely.

Her emotions were so tangled up with the Pantry that she found it difficult to sort through them. For an intense year, Peter had been the single focus of her life, and his sudden, incomprehensible defection had left her raw and bewildered in a world that seemed painfully aimless.

Time had helped give her perspective on her initial despair, but it had been the Panache Pantry that had made her pull herself together again. Once the idea had been nurtured, she had spent almost a year researching and planning the business. And then there had been the exhausting weeks of looking for exactly the right location. When James had shown her through the brand-new, untenanted arcade, she had known immediately it was the perfect spot. And it had been until Connan O'Rourke had shown up like the blight.

She attacked the last carton with her knife and began to pull out the faceted jars of brandied cherries. She couldn't decide what she detested most about

O'Rourke—his insufferable confidence or his deep, smoothly textured voice that made her think of a razor wrapped in velvet.

Chapter Three

The October morning was foggy, and it made the familiar landscape a little mysterious. Stray wisps of mist were caught in tree branches and tangled in the telephone wires overhead. Alicia eyed the pale light that filtered through the fog with a practiced glance and predicted that it would all burn off within the hour, leaving the day clear and bright. She slowed the van as she approached the turn to the château and felt an odd reluctance to go any farther.

She'd always looked forward to the first quiet hours of the day at the shop. It had always been her creative time, spent testing new recipes and planning her seasonal stock orders. Now she had to contend with Goliath's threatening intrusion into her orderly world. Her anticipation of the pleasant day ahead of her evaporated as Connan O'Rourke's image rose in her mind.

A tiny sigh escaped her lips. Damn the man! His presence was so pervasive that he was beginning to monopolize her thoughts. He pulled strings, and when his victims refused to dance, he resorted to veiled threats.

Her mouth filled with bitterness. Intrigue was not her normal style, but in this case it was more than justified. O'Rourke would swat them all as casually as flies if he found out what they were planning. She would have to make sure that Martha and the others understood the need for secrecy. Their most powerful weapon was going to be surprise, and they were going to need every advantage they could get if there was going to be a fighting chance to save the arcade.

The door of the shop was open, and Alicia could hear Richard's voice from the kitchen as she approached. She smiled as she heard him arguing about fruit over the phone. Richard was a wizard with purveyors. If there were any decent melons to be had, he would get them delivered to their door.

Richard concluded his conversation and ambled out to greet her. "I thought I heard you come in. Bernie swears on his mother's spaghetti sauce that his melons are fit for the gods."

"Well, that ought to satisfy the mighty O'Rourke."

"Do I detect a subtle note of loathing in your voice?"

"I don't like moguls, especially power-hungry, autocratic ones."

"Haven't you left something out?"

Alicia was confused. "What do you mean?"

"Like ruthless, depraved, lice-ridden and cannibalistic." He paused with a puckish grin.

Alicia grinned back at him. "Don't stop now. You're just getting the hang of it."

"I've got better things to do with my time. I've got to get started on Godzilla's cheese trays."

"That's Goliath, not Godzilla."

"What's a few scales between friends?" he shot back at her.

"Are you ever at a loss for a comeback? No, don't answer that. Listen, I've got to run over and see Martha for a few minutes and then I'll be back to break down the window display. Picnic baskets aren't exactly current in October."

"Fine. I'll give a shout if the lines get too long."

Alicia slipped into Martha's shop and shut the door behind her.

"What's up, Red?"

"That's what I was going to ask you."

"Well, not much. With the arcade closed yesterday, you and I were the only ones around. Today I haven't had a chance to collar anyone."

"Good. I've thought of something we didn't discuss yesterday. Martha, if this is going to work we've got to keep it as quiet as possible. If O'Rourke knew what we were up to, he'd find a way to stop it before we even got started."

Martha crossed her arms defensively across her chest. "I'm not *that* much of a gossip. I can keep my mouth shut."

"That's not what I mean. But when you talk to the other tenants, you'd better emphasize the need for secrecy. In fact, it'd be a good idea to try to get an idea of their reaction to the closing of the arcade before you mention a tenants' group at all."

Martha uncrossed her arms and nodded thoughtfully. "I see what you mean. Okay. I'll tiptoe around like a cat burglar."

A frown marred Alicia's smooth face. "I don't like being sneaky, but I don't see any alternative."

"I wouldn't let it bother you much," the older woman said philosophically. "Besides, if I know you, you probably told him where to go with his idea. He'd be pretty stupid not to expect you to do something about it, and I have a feeling that even though he's big, he's not dumb."

Alicia's face cleared. "You're right. He knows exactly how I feel about it. I won't waste any more scruples on him. I doubt if he knows what they are anyway."

"Good girl. I'll catch up with you as soon as I have anything to report."

Martha's dose of common sense was reassuring, and Alicia walked back to her shop feeling a lot more confident about the path she had chosen. She stood in the corridor and inspected her display window critically. The overflowing picnic hampers with the red, white and blue accessories had been attractive in August but were sadly out of place in October. She needed something to strike a seasonal note—maple leaves, or perhaps pumpkins.

She went in and started breaking down the display. Within an hour the floor in front of the window was piled with bottles and cartons. The only things left in the window were a half-dozen red, white and blue cheerleader's pom-poms that had been wired to the ceiling to suggest a fireworks display. She climbed up into the window and reached experimentally for one.

She wasn't even close and looked around in disgust for something to stand on. The folding chairs by the door looked just the right height, so she dragged one over and positioned it firmly under the pom-poms. By standing on her toes and stretching, she could just reach the wires and carefully began to untwist them.

Suddenly a large pair of brown hands spanned her waist, and she felt herself being lifted into the air and swung to the floor. "Are you trying to kill yourself? They don't call those things folding chairs for nothing." Connan O'Rourke's deep voice wrapped around her like rough velvet as he gave her a little shake to emphasize his words. She could feel the warmth of his hard hands through the cotton blouse she wore, and the separate pressure of each strong finger was distinct as it fitted into the smooth curve of her waist. As she stared into his gray eyes, some trick of light made them soften, and for a brief moment they seemed almost friendly. She shook her head, and the illusion disappeared. "Keep your hands to yourself," she spat at him, and pushed ineffectually at his chest.

His grip tightened, and he grinned down at her. "Now is that any way to treat the man who just saved your life?" His eyes skimmed her flushed face speculatively, bypassing her angry eyes to linger on the sculpted bow of her upper lip. "According to the old saying, you belong to me now." He removed one hand from her waist to trace the intriguing sweep of her cheekbone. "Now that's a pleasant idea. I can think of several things to do with a redhead." His hand moved to the full, silky curve of her lower lip, and Alicia felt mesmerized by his slow, deep voice and the rough slide of his thumb over her mouth. "Like this."

Before she could shake off the spell of his voice or anticipate his intentions, the dark head swooped down, and his lips were hot against her own. The contact only lasted a few seconds, but the intensity of it left her feeling as though she had been branded. He stepped away and looked at her quizzically and then stepped into the window and unfastened the pompoms. He thrust them into her arms and smiled as she fought to regain control over her vocal cords. Her first effort came out as an embarrassing squeak. "How dare you!" Then her voice returned to its normal pitch. "If you ever touch me again, I'll..."

"You'll do what?" he asked with obvious amusement. "Hit me? You're too short." Her eyes narrowed dangerously at his reference to her size. "Kill me? I don't think you could manage that either."

"You'd better stop laughing and start listening, you walking eclipse, because I'm only going to say this once. In case you hadn't noticed, your particular brand of mindless brawn went out several decades ago. Not only are you outdated and uncouth, but you are boringly predictable. If you try anything like that again, I'll make a scene like you've never dreamed of and I'll enjoy every minute of it."

A dangerous intensity replaced his amusement. She was all fire and response, and he found the combination lethal. The taste of her was still on his lips, and suddenly he was hungry for more. He frowned, but there was a devilish light in his eyes as he stepped closer and studied her angry face. "Boring? Yes, you could be right. Of course, I didn't realize you were expecting more."

He moved closer, and Alicia could feel his warm breath in her hair. He moved unexpectedly fast for so big a man, and before she knew what had happened, he had pulled her hard against him and covered her lips with his.

A heavy wave of warmth swept through her, leaving each separate nerve tingling and alert. She could feel the even rise and fall of his chest against her breasts, could feel the long, hard muscles of his thighs flex against her. In the back of her mind, a small, shrill voice sounded an alarm, but her body was too bemused by its own sensations to heed the hysterical warning.

His tongue tentatively entered her mouth, filling her with the inescapable taste and texture of him. His teeth scraped against the inside of her lower lip, and she found herself clutching at his shoulders as shuddering tremors chased down her spine. His hands were surprisingly light as they smoothed over her hips and traveled the graceful dip of her waist.

Her body became molten and flowing beneath his large, sure hands. He was sculpting her into a pliant, sensual creature who was totally unknown to her. The shrill warning grew louder, forcing its way through her sensually clouded mind, until her body stiffened in response.

Connan was aware of her withdrawal almost immediately. It was as if an arctic wind had blown into the room, lowering the temperature by twenty degrees. What had gone wrong? A moment ago she had been leaning into his hands, intoxicating him with the smooth heat of her body, and now she had gone all rigid and cold.

Alicia wedged a hand between their bodies and felt a bubble of hysterical laughter rise in her throat. She was still clutching a pom-pom and the bright red streamers drifted across O'Rourke's immaculate suit. She gave an experimental push and was gratified when his arms dropped. Risking a glance at his face, she found a ludicrous mixture of dismay and chagrin. The chuckle escaped her lips before she had time to consider its effect. His face darkened, and he took a step forward. She rattled the ridiculous pom-pom in his face and burst into unrestrained laughter. He looked so absurd wearing that grim expression with loose streamers clinging to his shoulders.

"You really should talk to your tailor. Somehow that ensemble doesn't strike the right note." She burst into fresh peals of laughter. "What do you call it anyway? The Mardi Gras seduction? I don't think I'm impressed."

He inspected his shoulders and brushed at the offending strands of red plastic as a reluctant smile lightened his features. "That's quite an arsenal you have, Alicia. Unlike you, I'm very impressed." His eyes lingered thoughtfully on her lips, which were still bright from his kiss.

She tensed immediately at the way he drew out the syllables of her name, making the sound of it a caress. "Why can't you take no for an answer?"

His smile was infuriating. "Is that what you were saying a few minutes ago? It sounded a lot more like yes to me."

"But we've already established that you have a problem understanding basic English," she retorted sweetly.

"I wasn't talking about English. I was talking about body language. Believe me, your body was definitely saying yes."

She felt the hot blood surge under her translucent skin and knew that he wouldn't miss her betraying reaction. Mentally she cursed her fair complexion, Connan O'Rourke and her own wayward responsiveness to him. For a few endless moments she had wanted to lose herself in the sensations he had called to life in her reluctant body.

"You're getting boring again, Mr. O'Rourke," she said through clenched teeth.

"They say that invective is the last refuge of a weak argument," he said musingly. "But never mind. I'll take your word for it. At least for now," he added. "As amusing as all this is, I actually came on business. James and I were going over the menu for tonight and have decided we'd like to add a hot hors d'oeuvre. Do you think you could manage something on short notice?"

Alicia blinked at his lightning-fast change of subject and found herself wishing that she was as facile. Her mind was still stuck halfway between the pompoms and the feel of his tongue filling the empty recesses of her mouth. "Something hot?" she repeated stupidly as she pulled her wandering thoughts back into line. "What about some crab-stuffed ravioli?" She suggested the first thing that came into her mind.

He nodded in easy agreement. "It sounds fine." Reaching for her hand, he uncurled her fingers and tucked a few red strands into her palm. "I'll see you tonight at six." He stepped through the door and paused to say over his shoulder, "And don't bother to bring your pom-poms. It's not that kind of party."

Inhaling deeply and counting to ten very slowly, Alicia managed to restrain the urge to toss the bundle of red streamers in his face. The man was unbelievbly efficient at getting under her skin. She rubbed the back of her hand over her lips, trying to scrub away the feel of him, but her blood still ran warm with the memory of his lips on hers. For a wild, impossible moment, she had wanted to respond, to become intoxicated with the sensuality that flowed from him like a sweet, heavy liquor.

O'Rourke was a master of technique, she thought disdainfully. No doubt he had plenty of hours of practice. She had been caught off guard once, but it wouldn't happen again.

Stepping carefully around a discarded picnic basket, she wondered idly why he had made the effort. Had he been merely amusing himself, or did he intend to disarm her hostilities over the arcade? It didn't make any difference, she decided. Shoddy bedroom games disgusted her, no matter what the motivation. O'Rourke had accomplished one thing with his Don Juan routine, though she was sure that it wasn't what he had intended: he had confirmed all her worst suspicions about him.

With a dismissing shrug, she walked back into the kitchen to let Richard know about the additional item on the menu.

"We're all out," he responded succinctly. "Remember? We used the last of it for the wedding reception on Saturday."

"Darn, I forgot all about it. When O'Rourke sprang it on me, I just suggested the first thing that came to mind. I guess I'll have to run into town and pick up some more at Tortellini and Company." Mentally she chalked up another black mark next to O'Rourke's name.

"Don't look so glum. It's not a tragedy. You'd have to go anyway to pick up your catering duds. I'll finish preparing the cold trays and get everything set up while you make like a silver bullet and fly."

Alicia smiled crookedly. At least one of them was thinking clearly. "Thanks, Richard. I'll put that window back together and then take off. I'll be as quick as I can. I know you want to get out early today."

Mable didn't fly, but the van did a good imitation of the speed limit on the way back to Portland and obligingly slid into a parking space right in front of the small specialty shop that manufactured fresh pasta. Alicia ran in and picked up the ravioli, and then, without examining her motives very closely, turned the van in the direction of a boutique that used to be located a mile or so down the road. She sighed with relief as she spotted the striped awning. The shop was still in business. It had been well over a year since she had stopped in even to look. Richard's casual reference to her catering duds had struck a nerve. Her green silk shirtwaist was about as imaginative as a uniform and almost as frumpy. If she was going to have to face O'Rourke again, she was going to do it in full battle armor.

She parked Mable and walked through the silver-and-green-painted door before she had a chance to change her mind. The woman behind the counter waved at her. "What are you looking for today? Something specific or just window-shopping?"

Alicia looked around at the colors and textures filling the small space and gave in to an irresistible urge. "I'm on a forty-minute shopping spree. The first thing I need is a cocktail dress for this evening—something restrained, but unforgettable. After that, you name it and I don't have it. Let's see how far we can get before I turn into a pumpkin."

"Into the dressing room and off with your rags then, Cinderella. This is going to be fun. I have the perfect dress for you. It's guaranteed to mesmerize any male within a half-mile radius."

Alicia slipped out of her sensible trousers and white blouse and hoped that the woman knew her business. It would be devastating at this point to be shown something in ruffles and bows. She wanted to look very sophisticated and in control tonight. The curtain rustled, and she looked up expectantly.

"My name is June, by the way. I just pulled everything off the rack that I thought would work with your coloring. This is the dress I was talking about. What do you think?"

It was electric blue and absolutely stunning. The skirt was a slim sheath, draped in the front and caught at one hip with a sparkling buckle. The bodice was fitted with long, narrow sleeves that ended in points at the wrist, and the high, snug collar buttoned asymmetrically down one shoulder.

"I'll probably look like a neon sign in that color, but I'm dying to try it on."

June dropped the dress over her head and helped her with all the tiny buttons at the neck. When Alicia turned to look in the mirror, she was stunned at the result. The top clung to the curves of her breast without being tight, and the high, pleated collar made her neck look long and graceful. The skirt was a work of art. When she took a step forward, the drape parted over her leg, revealing a glimpse of thigh quite a few inches above her knee.

"My, oh, my. Where are the safety pins?" Alicia muttered to herself.

June wagged a finger in reproof. "Don't even think of it. I won't sell it to you unless you promise to leave the skirt alone. I knew that color would be good on you. The contrast is dynamite against your skin and hair."

Alicia gazed at her reflection with satisfaction. The dress created exactly the effect she was after. She felt poised and confident, two more weapons in her armory against O'Rourke.

"I'll take it. We've got thirty minutes left. What other goodies do you have there?"

She tried on a black challis skirt splashed with mauve cabbage roses in a midcalf length, and June was able to match it with a delicate hand-crocheted sweater of a dustier mauve. There was a ridiculous pair of lavender corduroy slacks with a tight little vest and a pink-and-purple-striped flannel shirt. The colors were intoxicating, and she had to admit that June was right. She could wear stronger colors than the conservative navy and grays she was accustomed to.

"You are a miracle worker. I'll take them all and eat peanut butter sandwiches for the next two months."

"Just a minute. We've got five minutes left." June reached out and dangled a frothy handful of silk and lace in front of Alicia. "These just came in, and I have three in your size."

"These" were hand-embroidered silk teddies, one each of pale champagne, shell pink and black. They had tiny rows of tucks down the front and slender ribbon straps of picot-edged satin. The silk was sheer and fine. Alicia's passion for delicate lingerie trampled her budget into the dust. She adored the feel of silk next to her skin and reveled in the delicate femininity of lace and satin under her more prosaic clothing. "Make that peanut butter sandwiches for the next four months."

June wrapped the purchases in silver tissue paper and boxed them all while Alicia dressed. She was in a pleasurable state of shock at the amount of money she had managed to spend in the allotted forty minutes but knew that every penny was worth it. She smiled in anticipation of wearing the lovely things.

She had just enough time to stop at her apartment for a quick shower before starting back to Pheasant Run. She took the stairs two at a time, clutching the collection of dangling parcels in her arms. She tossed them all on the bed and pulled out the dress to inspect it for creases. It looked fine, apparently wrinkle proof.

She didn't have time to wash her hair, so she bundled it up under a shower cap before standing under the pulsating stream of hot water. In five minutes she was toweling the moisture from her body and dusting herself with a cloud of rose-scented talcum powder.

She hurried back into the bedroom, glancing at the clock and reaching for the package containing the delectable silk undies. She hesitated between the pink and the champagne. "Definitely not the black," she decided out loud. "After all, I'm working." She finally chose the champagne-colored teddy and sighed as it smoothed itself over her faintly flushed skin. She caught a glimpse of herself in the mirrored door of her closet and admired the artful fit of the deliciously frivolous garment. It skimmed low over her full breasts, sliding sensuously across her skin. An embroidered ribbon cinched it snugly around her waist, making it look tiny above the delicate flare of the fabric over her hips.

She pulled the pins out of her hair and tipped her head forward to brush the heavy cloud briskly before pulling the blue dress on. It slid in a thoroughly satisfactory way over the silk that purred next to her skin. After dealing quickly with her makeup, she leaned close to the mirror in order to fasten the innumerable buttons at her neck and shoulder, then grabbed her coat and took the elevator sedately down to the garage.

"Well, Mable, I see you're still a pumpkin. I should have talked to the fairy godmother about you as well as the dress," she said, glancing ruefully at the aged van. Her narrow skirt and high heels made climbing up into the high-perched vehicle something of a challenge, but she managed to scramble in without tearing her nylons. "If I wear this very often, I'm going to have to invest in an elevator for you, old girl."

The traffic had tangled itself into knots even earlier than usual, and Alicia fumed as she crept along at a snail's pace. She prayed that Richard would be his usual meticulous self in checking on all the last-minute details. She was going to be lucky to arrive before the wine buyers.

By the time she pulled into the parking lot, it was a quarter to six and her temper was in shreds. She raced into the shop to find it deserted, but Richard had left a pot of water boiling on the range. She unwrapped the ravioli and dumped it into the salted water and then reached for the phone to call the tasting room.

After one ring, her assistant answered. Alicia rushed into speech, "Richard, I got stuck in traffic and it took me an hour and a half to get here. Is the table all ready to go? I just threw the pasta into the pot and it should be ready in five minutes.''

"The table is all set up. I've got the chafing dish heating. The only thing out of control is our friendly landlord. He seems to think you left the country for Pago Pago or some equally inaccessible spot. I'll be right down to finish off the hot stuff.''

Alicia realized that she was still wearing her coat. She shrugged out of it and hung it up before wrapping herself in a big white apron. She tested one of the crab-stuffed squares and decided it was done just as Richard came barreling through the door. He grabbed the heavy pot from her and dumped the contents into a large colander to drain. "The sauce is in that other pan,'' he nodded. They worked together efficiently with a minimum of conversation and quickly finished the hot appetizer. Alicia stripped off her apron and headed for the door. "I'd better get to my battle station now.''

Richard gave a long, low whistle when he got his first unobstructed view of Alicia's elegantly draped figure. "Looks like you've declared war. If O'Rourke has any sense at all, he'll surrender immediately.''

She laughed, her good humor restored at his light compliment. She knew that she was looking her best, and the thought gave her confidence a hefty boost. "See you upstairs in a few minutes, and thanks for bailing me out again.''

Taking the slippery marble stairs as quickly as she dared in her spiky heels, she arrived at the tasting suite at exactly one minute to six. It was empty, and she breathed a sigh of relief as she walked to the far end of the paneled room to inspect the table. She really didn't need to bother. Her assistant was a pearl beyond price.

Not only had he arranged the trays of fruit and cheese with an artist's regard for shape and color, he had also remembered to place the cutlery and napkins out at convenient intervals around the table. She had a sudden thought and stood frowning at the basket of fresh strawberries in the center of the white cloth. She had forgotten to ask if the group wanted coffee at the end of the meeting.

O'Rourke entered the room as silently as a big cat and stopped short when he saw Alicia studying the buffet table. Relief lapped at him as he let his eyes travel over her tiny frame. He had been afraid that after the scene in the shop she wouldn't show up. The hot hors d'oeuvre had been a slim pretext to see her again, but he hadn't been able to resist the temptation. The rest had happened without forethought. It was probably the stupidest thing he had ever done, but he couldn't bring himself to regret it.

He couldn't stop staring at the burnished waves of hair that fell around her shoulders in a whispering cloud. As if his gaze had been an actual touch, she stiffened slightly and then turned slowly around to face him. The air caught in his throat, and he felt he was strangling as he drank in her loveliness. The vivid color of the dress played up the bright flame that circled her head and shoulders like living fire. The slim, elegantly draped fabric emphasized her graceful figure in a way that set his blood pounding through his veins.

She smiled remotely and walked toward him. As she moved, her dress parted with each step to reveal a slender length of leg gleaming like soft ivory among the darker, brilliant blue folds of her skirt.

"Mr. O'Rourke, I'm glad you're here. We forgot to ask if you wanted coffee after the tasting." Alicia was pleased with her control. She had obviously thrown him off-balance with her cool professionalism, and she enjoyed having the initiative firmly in her own hands. From now on she would think of O'Rourke as a big pothole, something that was only dangerous if you didn't know it was there.

He didn't miss the humorous quirking of her mouth and wondered what thought inspired the brief smile. He tried to imagine what a full, genuine smile would look like on her lovely lips.

Standing next to her dainty perfection, he suddenly felt stupid and clumsy. He couldn't even answer a simple question when she turned those deep green eyes on him full force. He dragged his staring eyes away and looked at the table behind her. "It looks great. You've done a terrific job. We probably won't need the coffee, but it wouldn't hurt to have some on hand in case anyone wants to indulge in a little caffeine."

"I'll run downstairs and get an urn then," she replied easily, and turned to go. His hand shot out and captured her arm. She frowned slightly, and he removed his hand slowly, searching for something to say that would keep her by his side. "Why don't you call down and save yourself some steps? The buyers should be here any minute, and I'd like you to be here to greet them. James did say that you acted as hostess for him."

She kept him in suspense for a moment as she considered the validity of his statement before nodding. "Yes, I suppose that would be all right. I'll just buzz Richard and ask him to bring it up." She moved toward the phone, and he found he was breathing in time to the steps she took. He shook his head and glanced at his watch. The evening was going to be interminable. In the space of a few minutes she had efficiently erased every tenuous personal thread between them. There had been no anger or animosity in her face, no embarrassment or self-consciousness. She was acting as if they were polite strangers.

His initial relief at her presence gave way to a surge of irritation at her indifference. Damn it. He knew she had been on the verge of responding to him. He had felt the quivering tension in her body when he'd held her. She couldn't be as impassive as she pretended, and he hoped she'd let him prove it to her, point by voluptuous point.

Richard arrived with the crab ravioli and then went back to the shop for the coffee tray while Alicia set up the hot pan in the chafing dish. She became aware of O'Rourke right behind her, not touching, but close enough for her to feel the heat of his body ignite the thin volume of air between them. She ignored his presence and leaned across the table to straighten a stack of napkins.

Connan cleared his throat to get her attention. "Alicia, the buyers just drove up. Will you come with me to meet them? By the way, you're looking stunning tonight. Thanks for being here."

She faced him and smiled artlessly. "I don't remember having a choice, but don't worry, I'll enjoy myself. I like talking to interesting people." She emphasized the word "interesting." They moved together to the hall and waited for the first arrivals. Alicia realized that she was indeed looking forward to the evening. Some of the guests were bound to be entertaining, and she found she was almost enjoying the presence of Goliath. Bemused at the thought, she glanced at the tall, rugged man beside her. But before she could examine her feelings further, the guests had arrived.

She shook hands with the buyers as they were introduced to her, quite relaxed about the interested attention she was attracting. She had met one of them at a previous tasting the year before.

His name was George Phillips and, although he was the head of a large distributing company, he talked like a gangster from a B movie. She tucked her arm in his once the stragglers were all safely inside the door and led him toward the buffet table. Despite his rough-diamond image, he was a man who appreciated fine food, and she wanted to get his reaction to the Northwest cheeses she had chosen to feature.

O'Rourke watched her progress across the room with irritation. If she needed that much support to walk in those ridiculous high heels, she ought to throw them out. She had tilted her chin up in response to some remark of George's, and he was struck by the cameo purity of her profile. Then she laughed a cascading chime that somehow filled the room and turned every head in her direction. Without volition, the men began to drift in her direction, using the food as an excuse to draw near. He gritted his teeth as she spread something on a cracker and teasingly fed it to George to the accompanying laughter of the group that was gathered around them.

What did she think this was, a party? These men were supposed to be here on serious business, and she had them acting like sophomores at a high school dance. He wondered at the game she was playing and then mentally reviewed the marital status of his guests with an eye to possible competition. He found himself scowling in the direction of a soft-spoken Texan who was standing unnecessarily close to her.

"I'm sorry, what did you say?" He reluctantly turned his attention to the gray-haired man who had just spoken to him for the second time.

"I said she's a real charmer, but I guess I don't have to point out that fact to you. If looks could kill, the cowboy would be pushing up daisies." The older man was obviously entertained by the spectacle.

O'Rourke frowned and pulled himself up short. If he didn't watch out, he'd be making a perfect fool of himself. He watched the Texan move even closer to Alicia and whisper something that made her laugh. Something powerful twisted inside him and, with astonishment, he recognized the emotion as jealousy. He had never seen her soft and receptive before. She was always either guarded or defiant when she was with him. Now he wanted something else. He wanted her warm and pliant against him, wanted her smiles and her soft caresses. He clenched his hands into hard, powerful fists. God, he wanted her to want him.

Chapter Four

O'Rourke murmured an excuse and strode across the room to the animated group around the buffet table. Under the force of his personality, the men parted before him, and he walked right up to Alicia. "May I have a few words with you, please?" he asked smoothly, and drew her into a quiet corner before anyone had a chance to protest. His hand slid up her arm and across her shoulders in a massaging caress. He caught a tantalizing whiff of roses as she walked beside him, and he could hear the whisper of her dress as it slipped against her body with each step she took.

"I'd like to begin the tasting now if you could help shepherd everyone to the table. We'll be tasting six wines due for release next month. I'd like to keep it fairly casual, so if you wouldn't mind pouring the first wine, the Chenin Blanc, we'll do the rest ourselves by passing the bottles down the table."

Alicia tipped her head back to meet his eyes and felt the familiar surge of annoyance at her lack of inches. O'Rourke's overgrown frame made her even more conscious than usual of her midget status. His eyes had grim little lines around them, and she wondered if he was concerned about selling the new releases. "I could pour all of the wines, if you'd prefer. The food won't take much attention at this point." Her voice was even and indifferent as she made the offer.

"I don't need you distracting everyone." His voice was harsh and grated along her nerves with the sensation of velvet being stroked the wrong way. "In fact, it might be more appropriate if you joined us at the table. You've certainly caught the fancy of most of the group."

"You're the one who insisted that I be here tonight," she reminded him sweetly. "Nevertheless, I wasn't trying to distract anyone's attention from your precious wines. I only meant to introduce George to his first sample of goat cheese, but everyone else seemed to be hungry and headed right for the table, too." She chewed her lower lip in agitation. O'Rourke obviously thought she had deliberately sabotaged his sales effort.

He took a deep breath and forced himself to relax. He was beginning to behave like a besotted sophomore himself. "I apologize if I've misjudged you. The sales tonight are critical, and I guess I'm on edge." He enveloped her hand in his own and stroked her soft palm with a circling movement of his thumb. "It doesn't matter, so don't look concerned. You've managed to put them all in an expansive mood and that means they'll be more amenable to buying. So

thank you very much and would you consider being
the official hostess the next time we do this?''

She found his quick change of mood confusing. At
first he seemed angry at the course of the evening so
far, and then he was eating her with his eyes. Now he
was paying her compliments and smiling at her in a
way that made her entire body tingle. "Haven't you
forgotten something?" she said lightly, and tugged at
the hand he still held in order to put some distance
between them. "If you have your way, Panache Pantry won't be at Pheasant Run." His face darkened, but
he ignored the taunt.

"Join us at the table." His words were halfway between a demand and a request. She shrugged and then
nodded, making the burnished auburn of her hair
come alive with the reflected light from the overhead
chandelier. He dropped her hand as if he had been
burned and turned away abruptly.

She returned to the group around the trays of nearly
demolished fruit and cheese and made a laughing
comment. O'Rourke heard one man retort, "A beautiful woman always stimulates the appetite." He felt
the now-familiar snarl of jealousy in his chest and tried
to ignore it as he placed an extra chair beside his own
at the head of the tasting table. Alicia had efficiently
turned the buyers toward the wine and was getting
them all settled.

He opened the Chenin Blanc and poured a small
amount into his glass to taste before handing the bottle to her. She moved around the circular oak table,
pouring a few ounces into each glass. O'Rourke
should have been watching the faces of the men who
could make the difference between a break-even season and a wildly successful one. Instead, he found his

eyes riveted to the intermittent glimpses of shapely thigh that her dress afforded him as she walked around the table. She returned to where he sat and leaned to whisper in his ear, "I'll be back in a few minutes. I need to straighten up the table and bring out the second round of trays."

Before he could insist she stay, she'd gone to the opposite side of the room where she moved the empty trays to a side table and replenished the supply of napkins. She lifted the phone and called down to the Pantry. "Richard, they've cleaned us out. Can you bring up the backup trays now? Then you can go home, and I'll clean up here when they've finished."

In a few minutes Richard slipped inconspicuously into the room with two more laden trays and deposited them on the table. Alicia smiled her thanks and then walked him to the door, stepping outside with him and closing the heavy panel of carved wood.

"How's it going up here? That table looked like army ants passed through."

"I know. For a while there I was afraid they were going to start on the tablecloth," Alicia replied.

"Do you think I should put together another tray, just in case?"

"I don't think we'll need it. They're starting on the wines now and will probably only do a little light nibbling at the break." She pushed her heavy hair back from her face and winced. The tiny buttons at her neck and shoulder had snagged in several locks, and she pulled at them impatiently. Richard looked at her with disapproval.

"If you keep that up you're going to lose both the buttons and your hair." He bent closer and applied his bony, competent fingers to the task of untangling her. "Stop wiggling. I've almost got it."

The door opened suddenly, and O'Rourke looked out at them. His inquiring expression faded when he saw how close they were standing, their heads almost touching. His dark eyebrows came together in a forbidding line as he watched Richard's hands move over Alicia's shoulder and come to rest at her neck. Anger swept through him as he watched her calm acceptance of the other man's hands on her body. "Isn't this spot a little public to indulge in tender scenes?" His voice cut through the air like a razor.

Richard jumped back as if he had been struck, a deep flush staining his face. "I was just...just..." he stuttered in confusion.

"Never mind, Richard. You don't have to explain anything. Mr. O'Rourke is just practicing his intimidation routine." She was furious at the condemnation in his voice and his presumption that she was indulging in an amorous interlude with her assistant. He had no right to act so superior, to make judgments about her behavior. Turning her back on his thunderous face, she placed her hand lightly on Richard's arm. "Thank you for everything. I don't know how I'd manage without you. I'll see you in the morning."

Richard cast an uneasy glance at O'Rourke and hunched his shoulders uncomfortably. "I could stay if you think you'll need me for anything," he offered tentatively.

"I don't think so," she answered coolly. "Everything is under control." She looked at the dark, forbidding man who was watching them like a hawk and added mockingly, "Except Mr. O'Rourke, of course."

Richard scurried away, relieved to be out of the line of fire, and Alicia turned to face O'Rourke with something very like exhilaration. It was about time for Goliath to swallow the fact that he couldn't bully her, and she was looking forward to jamming the lesson down his throat.

"Let's get a couple of things straight, Mr. O'Rourke. First of all I'm not answerable to you for my actions, so keep your gutter thoughts to yourself. Secondly, stay away from Richard. It took me too long to find him, and I don't want him upset by your ham-handed interference." She allowed her intense tone to soften and added with deceptive sweetness, "And thirdly, I think you've neglected your guests too long. After all, this isn't a morality review board. It's a wine tasting, isn't it, or had you forgotten?"

She swept past regally without sparing him another glance and reentered the room with a pleasant glow of triumph. Her eyes swept the table and automatically noted that the men had finished the Chenin Blanc and were now working on the Chardonnay.

She nodded at James Leandro, who sat in the chair next to the one that had been placed for her. "James, would you mind changing places with me?" She gave him a devastating smile. "I'd like to talk to George about that goat cheese." Her voice was low but perfectly clear and heard by everyone at the table, including O'Rourke.

"Lucky George," someone murmured.

O'Rourke's expression was bland as he pushed a glass of the wine in Alicia's direction, and his face betrayed none of the galling frustration he felt. Nothing had gone according to plan. He had lost control, and she had lost her temper. The hunger in him climbed to new heights, and she was farther away from him than ever.

O'Rourke drew his attention reluctantly back to the business at hand. "James, do you still think this Chardonnay will be an award winner?"

The winery's manager swirled his glass reflectively and took a slow sip of the golden liquid. "I'm sure of it. The extra time in oak has taken it right over the top."

There was an assenting rumble from other men at the table and several of them scribbled notes on the pads of paper scattered conveniently around the table.

"Do you want to open another bottle, or should we move on to the reds?"

The consensus was to get on with the red wines. As O'Rourke plied a corkscrew, the men took fresh glasses from the center of the table, and some of them wandered over to refresh their palates with bread and cheese before assessing the next round of wines. Alicia moved from group to group chatting knowledgeably about the wines, and when she saw that O'Rourke was ready to begin pouring, she moved back to the table, drawing all the strays with her. The gray-haired buyer watched Alicia with her retinue and nudged Connan. "How do you suppose she does that? She's got them acting like a pack of tame puppies."

For an unguarded moment, O'Rourke looked fiercely at the group, then he relaxed and smiled at the other man. "There's quite a woman in that tiny package."

They sampled the Merlot, followed by the Pinot Noir, and finished with a young but promising Cabernet. The buyers were enthusiastic with their plaudits, and James was almost rubbing his hands with glee at the astounding number of cases that had been ordered at the end of the evening. Alicia shook hands with all of them, accepting their compliments with grace, and went to begin the cleanup as O'Rourke escorted the group downstairs to the van that was waiting to carry them back to Portland.

With some insistent awareness, she knew to the second when O'Rourke reentered the room, although he hadn't made a sound. He watched her for a moment as she loaded a tray with the dirty glasses and then went quickly to her side. "Let me help you. You can't possibly carry that load wearing those heels."

"You'd be surprised at what I can do, Mr. O'Rourke, but thanks for the offer." She allowed him to carry the trayful of heavy glassware as she picked up the remnants of food left on the buffet table, and then they walked in silence to the freight elevator at the back of the building. In the kitchen Alicia directed him to put the glasses on a rack and push it into the dishwasher while she refrigerated the leftover cheese and locked up. When everything was cleaned up to her satisfaction, she reached for her coat and walked to the door.

Connan hesitated. The evening had begun careening out of his control ever since the moment he had glimpsed her vibrant face haloed by the incredibly sensuous clouds of her loosened hair. He had wanted to bury his face in it, breathing in the light, elusive fragrance that was uniquely hers. She had gotten to him in a way that no woman ever had. First, she'd enraged him with her casual affection toward Richard when she would scarcely spare him a civil word. Then she'd disarmed him with a grace and charm that had him reeling. He walked reluctantly to the door where she stood jingling her keys. He was beginning to feel desperate as she locked the door and began slipping into her coat.

He cleared his throat nervously, uneasy with the lack of his usual self-confidence.

"Alicia, thanks for everything tonight. The evening was wildly successful. In fact, I was afraid that James was going to start giggling he was so pleased with the orders we got from that group."

She looked at him without expression, and he almost stumbled over his next words. "Listen, I apologize for that scene in the hall. You're absolutely right. It was none of my business. How about a nightcap before we go? You didn't have much of a chance to relax tonight, and I'm sure it's been a long day."

Alicia looked at him carefully. The apology had been abrupt, but he sounded sincere. He stood in the doorway, his head barely clearing the frame. There was a peculiar tenseness in his posture, but he didn't look threatening, and he certainly wasn't trying to bully her. It had been a long day, sapping her both emotionally and physically, and the thought of a glass of wine before the long drive home was appealing.

Before she could help herself, she had accepted his invitation and found herself going back up the stairs at his side. In the tasting room she draped her coat over the back of a chair and sat primly at the table while a restrained O'Rourke poured two glasses of the lauded Chardonnay. He handed one to her and sat down across the table without saying a word. She twisted the stem of the crystal goblet in her hand as the silence at the table stretched endlessly between them. She finally took a sip and raised her eyes to his.

"Congratulations, you've achieved a really excellent wine here."

"Thank you," he said formally. His eyes darkened as they traced her lithe shape, and he stood up, abruptly turning away from her to stride restlessly around the room. Alicia watched him with a growing sense of uneasiness. He tipped his head back to drain his glass before pouring himself another one, and she watched in fascination as the muscles in his strong, corded neck contracted as he swallowed. His pacing brought him around to her side of the table, and suddenly her nerves began rustling like leaves before a storm. She pushed her hair back from her face and ran her fingertips along the back of her neck, trying to rub away the tension she felt.

"You're tired," he said, suddenly very close behind her. His hands were on the back of her chair, and she shook her head in silent denial. The vibrant curling strands brushed his fingers and seemed to twine and tangle in them. His hands clenched in an automatic reaction and then relaxed to slide under the curling mass and rest heavily at the base of her neck. "Let me massage that for you," he said in a voice so gruff it was almost unrecognizable.

Alicia tensed at the reaction his touch stirred in her and tried to lean away from his hands. "No, don't get up," he said in a deep soothing voice. "Let me do at least this much for you."

He pressed lightly against the slope of her neck and then slid his hands with long, slow strokes down her arms and back up again. It was a soothing motion, and Alicia found herself relaxing. His fingers buried themselves in her hair as his thumbs worked deep into the knotted muscles at the base of her neck. She gave a low moan and dropped her head. It felt so good—those strong fingers were melting away the kinks she'd hardly known were there.

O'Rourke's voice came from a long way away, "Is that the right place? I'm not pressing too hard, am I?"

"It's perfect." Alicia hardly recognized the throaty little voice that slipped past her lips. O'Rourke's fingers moved with unerring instinct over her muscles, in tune with the intricacies of her body. If she grew any more relaxed, her bones would begin to dissolve. An alarm sounded deep in her mind, and she told herself hazily that she was playing with fire. O'Rourke was too big, too close, too dangerous to let down her guard this way. If she let him get close, he'd find out how vulnerable she really was. But his hard, sure hands were magic against the tight muscles in her neck and shoulders, and surely a few more minutes wouldn't make any difference. She didn't notice exactly when the quality of his touch began to change, but somehow the delicious relaxation gave way to a languid warmth that had her ivory skin flushing.

His lips brushed her hair and then grazed her ear as he murmured, "I've wanted to do this all evening." He lifted the heavy weight of her hair and sank his face into its stubborn curls, entranced by the fragrance and texture of the living silk. Then he pushed the gleaming curtain to one side and fitted his lips to the curve of her neck beneath the high collar of her dress. Automatically she arched back, hungry for more of the delicious sensations that seeped through her body.

His breath was hot and damp through the thin fabric of her dress, and she felt herself longing for the intimate brush of his lips against her bare skin. The thought shuddered along her bones, obliterating all

rational considerations. His hands slid across her collarbone and grazed the tips of her breasts, forging a
smoldering path of sensation that took her breath
away. The alarms sounded more frantically this time,
but it was too late. He had pulled her to her feet and
tilted her face to his.

Her feelings of languor evaporated, to be replaced
by a longing so compelling that it was anguish. She
moved against him, and when their lips met, his
tongue darted into her mouth without any prelimi-
naries. As she welcomed the taste of him, a flume of
liquid desire shook her to the core with its intensity.
His kiss was deep and drugging, and she felt sus-
pended in space and time, conscious only of the flames
that licked at her. He lifted his head and said with awe,
"My God, Alicia, do you have any idea of what you're
doing to me?"

She could only shake her head mutely and press
herself against his body, needing the contact as desperately as she needed air. He sat in her chair and
pulled her onto his lap, holding her against the solid
planes of his chest.

His fingers worked slowly over the maddening buttons at her shoulders, and as each inch of creamy skin
was revealed, he paused to press his burning lips
against her for refreshment. When the last button was
undone, he smoothed the folds back and bent his dark
head to the vulnerable hollow between her breasts,
breathing in the scent of her warm skin. He shifted in
the chair and settled her more intimately in his lap so
that Alicia became frighteningly aware of how aroused
he was.

He made a sound deep in his throat and began an
exploration of the curves of her breast. She could feel

the abrasive texture of his jaw through the tissue-thin silk of her teddy, and her nipples became tight, painful buds in response. He welcomed the evidence of her arousal with a triumphant laugh and, pushing aside the silk, he traced an aching circle around each coral tip. He looked down at her, and Alicia went still at what she saw reflected in his eyes. They were alive with a fire that threatened to consume her. The fear that had lain quiescent under all the surprising sensuality of her response to him burst into renewed life.

What was she doing? What had she encouraged? With a strength born of desperation, she jerked away and practically leaped off his lap, clutching the bodice of her dress over her breasts.

O'Rourke stood up, looking bewildered. "Alicia." His voice was hoarse with passion. "What's wrong? Did I hurt you?"

His eyes narrowed as she backed away from him, fumbling frantically with the buttons at her shoulder. "No!" she said sharply, and then, as he moved toward her, "Stay away, just stay away."

He drew a purposeful breath and stood very still, as if he were made of granite. "What kind of game are you playing, Alicia? A minute ago you were warm and willing, and now you're playing the outraged virgin."

She closed her eyes, forcing the tears back with all her strength. "I'm not playing anything, and that's the point. For a minute I got carried away, and you can credit that to your excellent technique. But I'm not interested in playing bedroom games with you or anyone else."

His face was hard and ruthless, and Alicia thought she had never seen a man so dangerous in all her life. She shivered at the thought of how close she had come to putting herself in his power. Those mindless moments in his arms had brought her to the very precipice of surrender. Foolishly she had thought herself immune to the hungry, domineering type, to men like O'Rourke who only knew how to take. Apparently the lessons she had learned at Peter's harsh hands hadn't penetrated as deeply as she had believed. Her body had betrayed her with its unsuspected hungers, and she flushed at the memory of her own wantonness.

"Is that what you call it? Getting carried away? I can think of another, more honest motive. Was that the plan all along, to make me want you so badly I'd agree to anything, including scrapping my plans for the arcade?"

He was aching with frustration and a deep, bitter disappointment. "Too bad your little plan backfired. It was all your little digs about the arcade tonight that gave me the clue. Oh, I want you all right, but I'm not willing to pay the price. I don't like cheats."

Alicia's face went deathly pale at his insults. She clutched the edge of the table as her knees buckled, and for a desperate minute she thought she would faint. She was almost numb from the violence of his verbal attack. From some unplumbed reservoir of strength she pulled herself together and stumbled toward the door.

O'Rourke was appalled by the depths to which anger had dragged him. He stretched out a hand as she stumbled past, but she flinched and looked at him with such horror and loathing in her clouded green eyes that he didn't dare offer anything more. He didn't seem to have any control at all where she was concerned. His dark face paled at the enormity of his furious accusations. He slammed his fist into the solid

oak table. God, what could he do now? She was in no
state to drive herself to Portland, but she'd no doubt
cut her own throat before accepting any help from
him.

He ran to a window and looked out over the parking lot. A few minutes later he saw her slip like a
shadow toward her disreputable van and climb in. He
watched as she started the engine and turned the cum-
bersome vehicle toward the gate and then he ran down
the stairs to his own car. At least he could follow her
home, make sure that she arrived safely. Later he'd
find a way to apologize, to explain.

Alicia walked carefully into her apartment and
closed the door. The room was cold, and her hands felt
icy as she fumbled with the lock. She stumbled over to
the love seat and curled up in a corner, wrapping a
woolly afghan around her shoulders and tucking it
over her legs. She brushed away the tears that were
slowly overflowing onto her cheeks, but it was a
hopeless task. They came faster and faster as her body
was racked with deep sobs. What was wrong with her?
Why should O'Rourke's scathing contempt make her
fall apart? At least now he'd leave her alone. What did
the opinion of an accomplished womanizer matter?
Her tears flowed with renewed violence as misery
rocked her with unrelenting waves, and she cursed her
stupidity in allowing O'Rourke to steamroll himself
into her life.

She hugged the afghan around her shivering body,
trying to find some small comfort in its warmth, but
her thoughts swung back inexorably to the persistent
giant who had breached her painfully erected defenses. It had felt so good in his arms. The fierce ache

he had initiated in her body had faded somewhat, but she knew she would be reminded of his passion for days. He was another Peter, a taker who used and discarded women without ever giving anything in return. What kind of masochist was she to be attracted to that kind of man?

"My God, I want him," she whispered to herself, and then turned her head into the crook of one arm and let the tears rain down her pale ivory cheeks until she was drained. For the rest of the night, she sat curled up, staring sightlessly out of the window until the first pale streaks of dawn crept ghostlike into the silent, empty sky.

Chapter Five

Alicia tried to swing one cramped leg to the floor and groaned. It was locked in an aching knot and wouldn't work. She massaged it gently and was finally able to stagger into the bathroom. She turned on the shower and wearily dropped her clothes on the floor, then leaned toward the mirror to inspect her image. She was a wreck, her eyes swollen, her complexion splotchy and her hair wildly knotted. She looked at herself with disgust and turned to stand under the cleansing jets of water.

For long minutes she just stood there letting the steamy water warm her into a semblance of life and then she scrubbed herself fiercely, blotting out all thoughts of the previous evening's despair. Feeling a little more human, she wrapped a robe around her fragile-feeling body and padded in her bare feet to the kitchen to make coffee.

The familiar daily ritual helped to give her a sense of normalcy for which she was grateful. Rituals had been her salvation three years ago, nudging her gently through the long hours of every day—get out of bed, ten-minute shower, glance over the headlines of the morning's paper while the kettle boiled, make coffee and on and on. The accomplishment of each insignificant task had marked her slow progress out of the awful darkness and back into the light.

She had buried so much of what was intrinsically herself in order to please Peter, that by the time he had finally walked out there was scarcely anything left. She had felt like a cipher, a drifting mote without his shaping, directing hand at her back. She had almost forgotten how to be a person.

It had been a long, painful struggle to regain her self-respect and learn to be independent, and she had vowed at the time never to go through it again. One resurrection was enough for anyone.

Sipping her coffee as she walked down the hall to her bedroom, she was conscious of the frantic thoughts that boiled beneath her fragile surface composure. God, how could she face him again? How could she endure his contemptuous eyes? Buttoning the plain white blouse up to her chin, she glanced in the mirror and reached for a dark tie to knot under her collar.

He had been so tender and welcoming when she'd softened in his arms and then so frighteningly angry when she'd torn herself away. His anger was something she could understand. The memory of the way she had clung to him scorched her with humiliation. She had been dazed by the responses he had coaxed from her body with his large, gentling hands and, as a

result, had let things go much too far. She had be-
haved inexcusably, and she admitted that his anger
had been justified.

Her eyes hardened as she finished dressing, and she
ignored the pale thread of longing that wound through
her. Thwarted of an easy conquest, he had lashed out
at her cruelly. He had wanted to hurt her for not
wanting him. That was the man she would remember,
not the one disguised by a seductive facade of tenderness.

The shop was dark and the door locked when she
arrived. It was still quite early, and she was glad for the
respite from Richard's inquisitive presence. Her composure was thin at best, and she needed to get involved in some solid work, to refocus her mind and
energy. Looking at the hastily thrown together window display, she decided to start there.

By the time Richard sauntered in at seven-thirty, she
had finished the pyramid of imported olive oil cans
and was rearranging the ropes of garlic.

"Nice," he commented. "How'd everything turn
out last night? Did the ravening beast find a handy
Christian to eat?"

His irreverent comment brought a wry smile to her
lips. "Ravening beasts are sort of like the Mounties—
they always get their man."

Richard inspected her closely. "Don't you mean
woman? You look like hell. You should have let me
stick around."

Alicia was touched by his concern. "Don't worry
about it. Goliath just has a nasty temper."

"That's not news," he said caustically. "How about
a cup of coffee? Have you made any yet?"

"No, I wanted to finish this window so I could get started on those catering menus we wanted to mail out."

"Right. I'll get a pot started and bring you a cup when it's ready."

She watched his lanky form disappear into the kitchen and smiled affectionately. She was lucky to have an assistant who was both talented and compatible. Still smiling, she turned back to the display and leaned into the window to rearrange some bottles of herb vinegar. A sixth sense told her she was being watched, and she slowly raised her eyes, knowing in advance whom she would find.

On the other side of the glass stood O'Rourke, looking impossibly big. His eyes seemed to bore right through her and, as she watched, he moved slowly past the window and stepped into the shop. For a long moment he just stood there, staring at her with an enigmatic expression on his face. She couldn't tear her eyes away from his and had the distinct feeling that the ground had suddenly tilted under her feet and was sliding away.

"Alicia." His voice was very soft, but it shocked her out of her frozen immobility. She turned away and blindly pushed a basket of French bread into the window. She could feel him move closer and had to restrain a compulsive desire to jump into the window and cower behind the olive oil.

"Alicia." This time his voice had a definitely caressing note in it. For the first time in her life she was grateful for her short-fused temper. The man had an incredible amount of nerve. How dare he try out that bedroom voice on her after the things he had said last night? Standing very straight, she turned and looked at him with withering scorn. "You're in my way," she said, and brushed by him to retrieve a spool of plaid ribbon, which she proceeded to tie in elaborate bows around the stems of some small pumpkins.

His third attempt to get her attention had lost its smoothness and grated unpleasantly along her nerves. She hunched her shoulders uncomfortably and said without looking at his hard, chiseled face, "I'm busy, Mr. O'Rourke, and have absolutely nothing to say to you anyway."

"Don't be childish, Alicia. Things may have gotten a little out of hand last night, but you and I have lots of unfinished business to discuss."

She rounded on him fiercely, inflamed by his easy dismissal of a scene she had found so disturbing. "A little out of hand? How very urbane of you. I'm afraid I'm not in your league, Mr. O'Rourke, and I'm not interested in any more tryouts. If that's all you have to say, you can leave right now. I'm busy."

His face darkened at the contempt in her voice, and Alicia braced herself for the counterattack. He surprised her, however, and just stood there looking determined and unmovable. His voice was controlled and patient when he finally spoke. "You're obviously in no mood to listen to explanations, so I'll save them for later." He moved closer and cupped her chin in one hand, tilting it up so that he could see all the emotions that chased across her eyes. "But I'll tell you this, Alicia, and I've never been so serious about anything in my life. Last night was only the beginning between you and me."

Furious, she tried to shake her head in denial, but he ignored her and continued in a deep, drugging voice. "It's a pale word to describe how I feel, but I want you." He passed a hard thumb over the angry swell of her mouth. "And, though you're fighting the attraction between us, Alicia, I intend to see we both get our heart's desire."

He released her, and she felt as if her entire body were racked with tremors. Confused, she attributed the reaction to the anger coursing through her. He stood unmoved as she unleashed her temper and began to shout at him. "You overgrown, conceited behemoth. I'm going to make this simple so you'll be sure to understand. You are an unprincipled, low-life opportunist, and we have nothing to discuss."

He was not disturbed by her attack. "You're pretty good at that," he said with genuine admiration in his voice. "Come out to dinner with me tonight and I'll let you get in some more practice."

She clenched her fists and glared at him. "Get out. I'm dead serious."

"I can see that," he said sympathetically. "I'll pick you up at 5:45."

Without another word he left her seething impotently. Richard nudged her elbow and handed her a cup of coffee. "That was better than a soap opera," he said with amusement.

Alicia focused on his grinning face and asked, "Were you eavesdropping?"

"Of course not," he said with affronted dignity. "You two were making so much noise I could hear you back in the kitchen. Are you going to go?" he asked with undisguised curiosity.

"Since you heard everything, you must have heard my answer, too. Of course I'm not going. Why is everyone so obtuse all of a sudden? Isn't the word 'no' in your vocabulary either?"

"Don't get mad at me. I'm not as big as O'Rourke, and I don't think I'd survive one of your tongue lashings."

"Then behave yourself," she said more mildly, and smiled to take the sting out of her words. "Will you watch the shop? I've got to—"

"I know, you've got to go see Martha," he interrupted impishly. "What are you two cooking up these days? Every time I turn around you're scurrying off for another secret conference."

Alicia was startled at his question and looked searchingly at him. Had he somehow found out about the arcade and the tenants' group she was trying to organize?

"Don't look so worried. I don't know anything. But I'd have to be pretty stupid not to be aware that something is going on. The tension around here has been so thick you could cut it with a knife."

Alicia felt a twinge of guilt at keeping secrets from him. "I'll tell you everything as soon as I can," she promised, and left to consult with Martha.

"Who have you talked to?" she asked as soon as she was through the door. "And what did they think?" She was beset by a sudden sense of urgency to take concrete action against the autocratic O'Rourke. She had to show him how very serious she was in fighting him.

Martha eyed her tense, pacing form with disapproval. "Sit down and relax. You make me edgy just looking at you."

Reluctantly Alicia sank into a rocker and looked at her friend expectantly. "Well?"

"I talked to Ben and, as you might expect, he got himself all lit up over it. He was ready to call out the militia, and I had to spend some time calming him down. Henry Piper was shocked but nervous about making waves. He's going to think about it and get back to me later. Old Mr. Johnson was noncommittal but willing to come to a meeting. So that only leaves our jeweler, Mr. Larsen, who's away on a buying trip. I'll talk to him when he gets back next week."

Alicia sighed with frustration. "That means we won't be able to set up a meeting for at least another week."

"What's your hurry? I think I've done pretty well," Martha said with a slightly defensive note in her voice.

"You have. In fact you're a marvel. It's just that O'Rourke is getting to me. He's so sure of getting his own way that I can hardly wait to throw up a roadblock. The man infuriates me." She paused and then added, "Besides, I think the arcade is worth fighting for. We've all worked too hard to give it up so easily."

"Sounds to me like fighting the giant is more important to you than fighting for the shops."

Alicia laughed uneasily. Martha's comment was a little too perceptive for comfort. "Of course not. You know how I feel about the Panache Pantry. But I admit that seeing Goliath stumble would give me a lot of satisfaction."

Martha raised her eyebrows at Alicia's admission, but didn't comment further. "Why don't we tentatively schedule a meeting for a week from Sunday? That'll give me plenty of time to talk to Larsen when he gets back and fill him in on all the details."

"I guess that's the best we can do," Alicia agreed, not bothering to conceal her impatience.

* * *

After adding a few finishing touches to the window, Alicia settled down at her desk and concentrated on the mailing list. Richard whistled cheerfully in the background as he trimmed and chopped vegetables for a marinated salad, and she began to doggedly address flyers. Whenever O'Rourke's arrogant image drifted before her eyes, she would redouble her speed, until by the end of the day nearly two hundred were ready for the mail.

"Closing time," Richard said from the shop door.

Alicia stretched her stiff arms and looked at her watch. It was three o'clock, and O'Rourke had been conspicuously absent all day. She hadn't taken his threat to pick her up seriously, but on consideration she decided to play it safe. After all, her address was in the phone book where any madman could find it.

She'd close up the shop, mail the flyers and then window-shop until well past O'Rourke's decreed time of arrival. Forty-five minutes of heel-kicking would convince even him that she wasn't going to show. Then she could go home to some well-earned solitude and tranquillity.

"I'll see you tomorrow, Richard. I'll mail these this afternoon, and with a little luck we'll start getting some calls about holiday catering."

"I don't see how we can miss with your brawn and my pretty face." He pursed his mobile features into an exaggerated simper and minced out.

Alicia turned out the lights, and with a nervous glance down the corridor, locked the door and headed for the parking lot. It was ridiculous to feel so apprehensive, she lectured herself sternly. Nevertheless, she was only able to relax when she had put several miles between herself and the château.

In the post office she spent forty minutes sticking stamps on the mailers. Having them metered would have been a lot faster, but she was determined to stay well out of O'Rourke's way. She remembered the set of his jaw when he'd said that he would pick her up at 5:45. His damn ego was a mile high. Her skin warmed uncomfortably when she recalled his other, even more outrageous statement, and she wished passionately that she could have dismissed it as a total fabrication. With brutal honesty, she admitted to herself that she had responded to him, that she had welcomed his hands and lips on her body with a hungry desperation she found frightening, even in memory.

She shook her head to clear the disturbing images and bundled her folders into the mail drop. Battling the downtown traffic as it geared up for rush hour, she turned into a department store parking garage and prepared to kill a couple of hours. Starting in the basement, she perused discontinued sheet patterns and budget towels. Then she moved through housewares where an ingenious cherry pitter held her attention for several minutes. Methodically she worked her way through better furniture, cosmetics, accessories and shoes before collapsing on a chair in the book department.

Lord, she had never realized how exhausting looking could be. She checked her watch and groaned when the hands stayed coyly at six o'clock. Damn O'Rourke. She hoped he had been serious about dinner and was furiously pacing outside her door at that very moment. She settled herself more firmly in her chair and vowed not to budge until six-thirty at the very earliest. Twenty minutes crawled by, and she finally stood up, admitting she couldn't take it anymore. She cursed him again before moving slowly in the direction of the garage.

As she edged Mable into the heart of the commuting tangle, she reflected gloomily that O'Rourke probably hadn't been anywhere near her apartment and that her self-inflicted torture had been needless. He was probably sitting in his luxurious leather chair at the château at that very moment, enjoying a hearty laugh at the way he had made her scurry for cover.

By the time she reached her apartment building, resentment, anger and several other less definable emotions had snarled her thoughts into a maddening spiral that began and ended with the picture of O'Rourke's dark face leaning close to hers and looking intently into her eyes.

She pulled into her normal parking place by the elevator and looked around the garage for any unfamiliar cars before getting out. Everything looked exactly the way it always did, and Alicia began to feel silly about the elaborate evasion. In the elevator she jingled her keys impatiently. She was longing for a shower, and her stomach was actually growling. She hadn't eaten all day, and she was starving.

The elevator doors slid open, and her heart slammed into her stomach. O'Rourke's eyebrows quirked devilishly as he plucked the keys from her nerveless fingers. "Right on time, I see. Let me get the door for you."

She stood in the middle of the hall and watched in horrified disbelief as he sauntered to her door, unlocked it and walked in. Numb with shock, it took her several minutes to pull herself together enough to follow. He was sprawled comfortably in her love seat, paging through the morning's paper. He looked up briefly when she entered the apartment. "You'd better hurry if you want a shower. Our reservations are for seven-thirty."

"Get out."

"I think you'll like this place. It's small and cozy and has a nice view of the river. Some friends of mine own it."

"I'm not going anywhere with you. Didn't you get the message when I wasn't here at 5:45?"

His smile was disarming, and his voice projected innocent dismay. "Did I say 5:45? How careless of me. I meant 6:45."

Alicia looked at him bitterly as she realized that she had been outmaneuvered by a master strategist. She sank into a chair and stared glumly at her feet. "I suppose you think this is absolutely hilarious."

He put down the paper and leaned forward, suddenly deadly serious. "No, Alicia. I'm having a hell of a time trying to find any humor in this situation at all. You and I have to talk, and that's what we're going to do. So why don't you give up gracefully and go get ready?"

"Don't give me orders and don't patronize me." Her voice rose, and she stood up to face him. "Get out. How many times do I have to say it? Get out of my apartment. Get out of my life and leave me alone."

He stood up slowly and seemed to fill the small room with his broad shoulders and long, muscular legs. "Patience has never been my long suit, Alicia, and you've just about exhausted mine. I'll make a bargain with you. Come with me now, and after din-

ner you can call the shots. If you tell me to get lost, I'll
head for Siberia without a compass."

A small trickle of relief eased the unbearable tension in her body, and she looked at him assessingly.
"How do I know I can trust you to keep your word?"

His face hardened at the implied insult, but his voice
was reassuring. "I always keep my word."

She searched his face again for deceit and was satisfied at what she found there. "It's a deal. Give me
fifteen minutes to get ready."

Alicia stepped into the shower and let the hot water
cascade down her back. Was she being a gullible fool
in trusting O'Rourke? Her options were so limited that
she decided it didn't matter.

She toweled the moisture from her body and
wrapped another towel around her head before slipping on a robe and padding down the hall to her bedroom. She opened the closet and surveyed her limited
wardrobe. She wasn't going to wear the cocktail dress
again. Finally she yanked out an old turquoise angora sweater dress. It was the only other thing that was
suitable, and at least it covered every inch of her body
with its long sleeves and turtleneck collar. She didn't
want to take a chance on being thought provocative.
It took only a few minutes to finish dressing and ap-
ply a minimum of makeup. She slipped into a pair of
spiky high heels, fluffed her still damp hair with her
fingers and rejoined O'Rourke in the living room.

When O'Rourke's strained senses caught the soft
sounds of Alicia's movement back down the carpeted
hallway, he dropped his eyes to the newspaper in his
hands. He couldn't allow her to see his hunger or the
intensity of his resolve just yet. It would only frighten
her, and he had done enough of that already. He was

HIT·THE
JACKPOT
WITH
SILHOUETTE

THE JACKPOT

Scratch off the 3 windows above to see if
you've HIT THE JACKPOT

If 3 hearts appear, you get an exciting
Mystery Gift in addition to our fabulous
introductory offer of

**4 FREE BOOKS PLUS
A FOLDING UMBRELLA**

PEEL UP STICKER AND MAIL TODAY

IT'S A JACKPOT OF A GREAT OFFER!

- 4 exciting Silhouette Romance novels—FREE!
- a folding umbrella—FREE!
- a surprise mystery bonus that will delight you—FREE!

Silhouette Folding Umbrella— ABSOLUTELY FREE

You'll love your Silhouette umbrella. Its bright color will cheer you up on even the gloomiest day. It's made of rugged nylon to last for years, and is so compact (folds to 15") you can carry it in your purse or briefcase. This folding umbrella is yours free with this offer.

But wait . . . there's even more!

Free Home Delivery!

Subscribe to Silhouette Romance and enjoy the convenience of previewing new, hot-off-the-press books every month, delivered right to your home. Each book is yours for only $1.95. And there's no extra charge for postage and handling!

Special Extras—Free!

You'll also get our free monthly newsletter—the indispensable insider's look at our most popular writers and their upcoming novels. Now you can have a behind-the-scenes look at the fascinating world of Silhouette. It's an added bonus you'll look forward to every month. You'll also get additional free gifts from time to time as a token of our appreciation for being a home subscriber.

TAKE A CHANCE ON ROMANCE—
COMPLETE AND MAIL YOUR SCORECARD
TO CLAIM YOUR FREE HEARTWARMING GIFTS

If offer card below is missing, write to:
Silhouette Books, 120 Brighton Road,
P.O. Box 5084, Clifton, NJ 07015-9956

PLAYER'S SCORECARD

MAIL TODAY

4 FREE BOOKS

FREE FOLDING UMBRELLA

Did you win a
mystery gift?

Place sticker here

Yes! I hit the jackpot. I have affixed my 3 hearts. Please send my 4 Silhouette Romance novels free, plus my free folding umbrella and free mystery gift. Then send me 6 books every month as they come off the press, and bill me just $1.95 per book, with no extra charges for postage and handling.

If I am not completely satisfied, I may return a shipment and cancel at any time. The free books, folding umbrella and mystery gift remain mine to keep.

CJR 037

NAME _____

ADDRESS _____

APT. _____

CITY_____

STATE _____

ZIP CODE_____

SILHOUETTE "NO-RISK" GUARANTEE

• There is no obligation to buy—the free books and gifts remain yours to keep.
  • You receive books before they're available in stores.
  • You may end your subscription anytime—just let us know.
  Terms and prices subject to change. Offer limited to one
  per household and not valid for
  present subscribers.

DETACH AND MAIL CARD TODAY

PRINTED IN U.S.A.

Mail this card today for
4 FREE BOOKS
this folding umbrella and
a mystery gift ALL FREE!

BUSINESS REPLY CARD

FIRST CLASS PERMIT NO. 194 CLIFTON, N.J.

Postage will be paid by addressee

Silhouette Books
120 Brighton Road
P.O. Box 5084
Clifton, NJ 07015-9956

NO POSTAGE
NECESSARY
IF MAILED
IN THE
UNITED STATES

almost sure that she had been hurt by someone in the past and had built some formidable barriers as a result. Somehow he had to regain her trust, and it was going to take gentleness and endless patience. He smiled sardonically at the thought and willed his clenched fingers to relax. Patience was one of his rustier virtues.

She hovered tentatively in the doorway and then joined him in the living room. The bright turquoise of her dress intensified the green of her eyes and provided a startling contrast to her loosened cloud of sunset-colored hair. The dress itself was demure, but its effect on him was not. The soft knit followed her lithe curves seductively, and the angora was a tactile invitation that made his whole body clench in frustration. He put aside the newspaper he had been pretending to read and stood up.

"That color suits you," he said matter-of-factly. "You're beautiful."

Alicia's response was suspicious and rigidly polite.

"Thank you," she said shortly. "Shall we go?"

She ran one hand through her hair and casually pushed it away from her face before turning to pick up a small envelope clutch. O'Rourke's large hands jammed themselves into his pockets. The temptation to run his own hands through her heavy curls was almost irresistible. She was seducing him with every unconscious gesture she made. His self-imposed restraint was going to be more difficult to maintain than he had expected.

He reached over her shoulder to help her with her coat, and her eyes flashed in annoyance at his proximity. Even in her heels, he made her feel like a dwarf. She let her emotions simmer for a brief moment and then reluctantly accepted his offered assistance. She had to get through the evening as smoothly as possible. Then, with a little luck, she'd never have to deal with him again or with the unwanted emotions he stirred to life inside her. The thought should have brought a sense of triumph or relief. Instead she suddenly realized that she was dismayed by the possibility of never seeing him again. Confused, she forced the unwanted realization to the back of her mind.

They walked silently toward his gleaming green Porsche, which was parked around the corner. He unlocked the door and helped her in before going around to the other side and somehow folding his large frame to a size the bucket seat would accommodate. He started the engine, and they drove into the sparkling cold city night.

In the close confines of his luxurious sports car, she could smell the clean soap and water scent of him and the faint tang of a woodsy after-shave. His hands were callused, she noticed for the first time, but scrupulously clean, and she wondered how he'd come by those marks of manual labor. She realized that she knew next to nothing about him except that he owned Pheasant Run, wanted to get rid of the arcade and was attracted to her. That's all you need to know, she told herself sternly. You're here under duress tonight, remember. Listen to his routine, point him toward Siberia and get out fast.

Despite the forced stridency of her thoughts, she found it impossible to ignore the tingling awareness in her body. She was too conscious of O'Rourke's muscular thigh so close to her own, too disturbed by the faint currents of air that seemed to wrap around her each time he drew a breath and exhaled into the intimately confining space they shared. She pressed her cheek against the cold glass of the window and stared sightlessly at the passing buildings. If she could just get through the next few hours, she would be free of him. He had promised, and all she had to do at the end of the evening was to tell him she never wanted to see him again. She would be finally free of his attempts to charm her into his bed. Surprisingly the prospect brought her little comfort and caused something to coil protestingly inside her.

"Earth calling Alicia. Are you there, Alicia?" He teasingly brought her attention back to him. She shook her head and absentmindedly ran her hands through her hair. He was beginning to watch for the gesture, remembering the way her hair had wrapped around his own fingers like something alive.

"Are we there? Where is the restaurant?" Alicia looked at him suspiciously. All she could see was a neatly painted gray house with wide steps to a brightly illuminated old-fashioned porch.

"Right there," he said, and nodded at the house. "The owners converted the main floor into a small dining room. Joan does the cooking, and Paul does all the organizational stuff. I guarantee that you're going to have the best meal of your life. Come on, let's go in."

He came around to open the car door for her and offered his hand to help her out. He retained his grasp as they walked up the stairs, her delicately boned hand swallowed up by his hard, callused fingers. She could feel the not unpleasant rasp of his skin against her own, softer flesh and couldn't repress a shiver of reaction. He opened the carved oak door, and they found themselves in a large hall with highly polished parquet floors covered with a durable looking braided rug. The walls displayed a varied collection of antique mirrors, and several old high-backed church pews provided seating for the two couples who were obviously waiting for a table. O'Rourke moved toward a small desk at the far side of the room, exerting a gentle pressure to keep her close to him.

"Alicia, I'd like you to meet Paul Morgan, the talented proprietor of this charming establishment. Paul, this is Alicia Stevenson who owns the Panache Pantry in the arcade of the winery."

Alicia's eyes widened. So this was the fabled Morgan and Morgan's. The name had filtered through even her preoccupation with the shop. People who were lucky enough to get a reservation spoke of it in hushed voices as if it were a newly discovered masterpiece by da Vinci.

"It's nice to meet you, Alicia. Your table is all ready. Let's get you two settled."

She liked him immediately. He was open and friendly in a casual sort of way, not at all the haughty, award-winning restauranteur she would have expected. They followed him into a cozy, paneled room that contained a massive stone fireplace with a crackling log fire. The flames were reflected in antique mirrors and the bank of casement windows that lined one wall.

Paul led them to a corner table flanked by two burgundy velvet wing chairs and invited them to sit down. There was a bottle of champagne chilling in a frosty silver bucket and hand-lettered menus at each place. As Paul opened the wine with a discreet pop and poured it into the slender crystal glasses, she gazed out the window in silent appreciation of the magnificent panorama below. The river was a ribbon that was spangled with the reflected lights of the city. It was even more beautiful because it was so unexpected in this unassuming house tucked into the side of a hill. She turned back to O'Rourke and found him laughing at some remark of Paul's.

"I'll check back with you later. Joan will want to say hi after the dinner rush dies down."

Alicia looked at the smiling, relaxed man opposite her with new eyes. There was nothing hard or threatening about him now, and she realized that she was seeing a side of him that she hadn't suspected even existed. Away from the arcade with its conflicts and tensions, he assumed much more human proportions. Suddenly it seemed the most natural thing in the world to be sitting across the table from him. The emotional tension that had punctuated their relationship from the very beginning faded from her mind. The sensual awareness was still there, of course. She doubted if she'd ever be totally free of that, but it was simmering in a well-behaved way in the background. She felt her confidence return. He seemed to be on his best behavior, and she resolved to do the same. There was no reason they couldn't be civilized about the whole thing.

O'Rourke raised his glass, and she joined him in the toast he offered, "To the unexcelled food, wine and company."

She took a sip from the delicate crystal glass and looked curiously across the table at him. "Not Pheasant Run champagne?"

"I hate to be disloyal to my own product, but we can't compare to the premium-grade French imports yet. After all, we've been making it for only two years, and they've been doing it for hundreds. That's a bit of a head start. But I'm confident that, given a little more time to perfect our methods, we'll be able to give them a run for their money.''

She took another sip of the sparkling wine and leaned back against the velvet upholstery. The chairs were actually comfortable, unlike typical restaurant seating. O'Rourke picked up the menu and ran a familiar eye over the list.

''What are you hungry for tonight? Duck glazed with apricot sauce, steak sautéed with red wine and shallots, or how about fresh filet of halibut?''

Alicia responded to his light manner and picked up her own menu. The list was not extensive, but each item was designed to appeal to the senses. She caught the faint whiff of butter and garlic as a waiter carried something by in a large covered tureen. She checked the menu and decided it must be the steamed mussels. She glanced up at him and said, ''It all looks marvelous, and I'd like to try everything. How about sharing a bucket of mussels with me while I make up my mind? That way my choice won't be unduly influenced by my growling stomach.''

The appetizer was ordered and delivered with dispatch. When the waiter removed the lid from the heavy pottery bowl, a cloud of redolent steam was released. She took her cocktail fork and reached for one of the shining blue-black shells with a dainty greediness. Her uninhibited enjoyment was obvious as she dipped the fragrant morsel into hot garlic butter and carried it to her lips. O'Rourke held his breath as she brought one tapered finger back and licked it with the unconscious delicacy of a cat. He found her incredibly sensual. Without thinking, he took his own fork, speared a plump mussel and, reaching easily across the table, slid it into her mouth. She was shocked at the unexpected gesture and looked at him warily.

"I can manage to eat them quickly enough on my own, you know." She reached for another shell, but he captured her hand and held it tightly.

"Let me, I'll save you the sticky fingers," he replied gruffly.

Alicia was mesmerized by the slow play of his hand between the mussels and her mouth. He alternated bites with her, first taking a mussel for himself and then feeding one to her. He pulled the fork slowly from between her lips each time, catching the soft inner tissue and making it tingle. She wasn't looking at his face any longer but followed the path of his hand as it came closer and brushed carelessly along the line of her jaw. When the mussels were done, he brushed a drop of the melted butter from her full lower lip and carried it to his own with an intensely intimate gesture. She could scarcely tear her eyes away from the message in his eyes and belatedly realized that she was being seduced.

"Stop it," she whispered.

"I have. They're all gone," he replied with mock innocence.

"That's not what I mean and you know it." She picked up the menu and hid her slowly burning face behind it. I must be intoxicated, she thought, and resolved to refuse any further champagne.

"Alicia," he said caressingly, "you'll be able to read that better if you turn it the other way."

She realized that she had been holding the menu upside down and was forced to meet his laughing face with a rueful smile of her own.

"I'll have a spinach salad and the halibut in brandied cream," she said firmly. He signaled for the waiter and gave their order, adding a request for a bottle of Pheasant Run Chardonnay. The waiter filled their glasses with the last of the champagne, and she pushed hers resolutely aside as she drew a deep, steadying breath. Her senses were swimming, and she perceived a new vulnerability in herself. O'Rourke the domineering autocrat had been difficult enough to deal with, but at least she had anger as a shield. This amusing, considerate man with the soft, sensuous message in his eyes totally disarmed her. He was making every effort to charm her, and she had to admit that he was succeeding.

The rational part of her warned her to be suspicious of his motives, to watch every step he took. Peter had been the most charming man of her acquaintance, and he had wielded that practiced, rapierlike charm with deadly precision. At twenty-one she hadn't been able to recognize that his strength had fed on her weakness. Now she was both older and wiser, and she knew that she ought to withstand O'Rourke's insidious charm. But a yielding, feminine part of her stirred and urged her to respond.

Chapter Six

The waiter appeared with their salads and made a small ceremony of grinding fresh black pepper over the plates before disappearing again. Alicia looked at the beautifully arranged bouquet of tender green spinach leaves and exotic enoki mushrooms. It was a visual masterpiece, and more than that, it was an excuse to avoid O'Rourke's searching gray eyes. She knew her own were transparent, that he'd be able to read the longing and indecision there.

"Relax, Alicia, I'm not going to eat you." His voice was light and teasing.

"Are you sure? I feel like I'm going to be your next meal every time we're together. You're like a hungry lion ready to pounce."

She'd matched his light tone, but O'Rourke knew that despite her amiable pose she was still on the verge of flight. He summoned a smile from some untapped reserve and said gently, "I apologize. Let's enjoy our dinner. Paul and Joan would never forgive me if we didn't do justice to their food.''

Alicia managed a smile in return and picked up the chilled fork that had been provided with the salad. She was grateful that he had defused the situation with humor but was at the point where she couldn't trust herself, let alone him. She eyed him warily over a bite of salad but saw nothing in his expression that she could take exception to. She took another forkful of salad and belatedly recognized the texture of ground walnuts in the raspberry vinaigrette dressing. She would concentrate on the food, she thought; it was a lot safer than the disturbing giant sitting opposite her. She finished her salad with enjoyment, mentally speculating on the ingredients of the dressing.

''The reviewers were right for a change. That salad went right off the scale,'' she said, attempting to break the charged silence that had built up between them.

''Wait till you taste the rest. Joan is a genius.''

''You seem to know them well. Do you eat here often?'' She cringed at the triteness of her remark.

''I went to school with Paul. We've been friends for a long time.''

''You said Joan prepares the food. Do you know where she got her training? She has the hand of a master.'' Alicia risked a glance at him and then shied away from the warm amusement in his eyes.

''She went through the Culinary Institute program and then apprenticed in a small nouvelle cuisine restaurant in California. We'll go back into the kitchen after dinner and you can meet her if you like.''

''Really? I'd love to.'' Alicia glowed with enthusiasm at the idea, and all her cool restraint evaporated. O'Rourke allowed himself to hope that the evening might yet be salvaged. She was all volatility and quicksilver charm, a retreating prize that moved farther away with his every effort. He became aware of the interested glances she was attracting from the male half of the diners who shared the room with them. Unconsciously he hitched his chair closer to her to make his claim clear. The waiter materialized at that moment and efficiently rearranged the flatware to accommodate his new position.

"The light was in my eyes," he mumbled in explanation.

The waiter looked surprised at the statement but didn't say anything as he presented the two plates for their inspection.

O'Rourke leaned close to refill her wineglass, and Alicia found herself tensing. She didn't want to breathe in the scent of him, didn't want the brush of his arm on her shoulder or the warm, intimate exhalation of his breath on her cheek. The evening was beginning to remind her of a fencing match she had watched in college . . . advance, retreat, parry and thrust. She cursed herself for letting her guard down and allowing him to feed her the mussels. Any small compliance on her part was sure to be misinterpreted, but she seemed caught in a soft, fragile spell.

He settled back in his chair, and she turned her attention to the food before her on the starched white cloth. The halibut was cooked to perfection, moist and flaky in the rich cream sauce. O'Rourke had chosen seafood, too. The aroma of his broiled salmon with fresh basil butter teased her already stimulated senses.

"How is your salmon?" she asked, trying to maintain the facade of normality. "This halibut is worth dying for."

"Perfect, as usual. Do you want to try a bite?"

She shied instinctively from the offer, but O'Rourke seemed to read her mind as he sliced off a portion and placed it neutrally on her bread plate without waiting for an answer. Giving in to a sense of inevitability, she allowed herself to relax and simply enjoy the moment.

Connan watched her unobtrusively. The graceful movements of her small white hands fascinated him, and he allowed himself to fantasize about them moving like butterflies on his body. His mind flooded with remembered sensation—the liquid satin of her mouth, the exciting contour between her narrow waist and the firm flare of her hips, the salty-sweet taste of her skin, the magic of her kiss.

Desperately he tried to turn his thoughts into less torturing channels. "Alicia," he said thickly. She looked startled, and he realized that his tension must have been evident in his voice. He took a deep breath and forced himself to continue in a blandly conversational tone. "Are you the homegrown variety or a transplanted Oregonian like Paul?"

Alicia gave a tiny sigh of relief. For a moment she had felt threatened again, but the innocuous question set her at her ease. "Definitely the homegrown variety. I was born and raised in Eugene along with my unruly pack of older brothers."

"So you come from a large family—I've always thought that would be fun."

Alicia looked at him appraisingly. "You're obviously from a small family if you think that. I was the youngest and the smallest and a girl besides. The boys could make me miserable and frequently did."

"But it wasn't all bad, was it?" He continued to probe.

"Of course not," she said quietly, trying to think of a polite way to change the subject. She disliked talking about the past and skirting around disquieting memories. A glance at his intent expression assured her that he wouldn't just drop his line of questioning, so she decided to give him a capsulated version of her childhood.

"As early as I can remember, I was tagging along after my four older brothers. They were all tall and athletic, while I was considered, in their kinder moments, to be the runt of the litter. I was always underfoot and I suppose they considered themselves very forbearing to put up with my presence. Gradually, I became a sort of mascot for the whole gang they ran around with."

Connan said thoughtfully, "That doesn't sound so bad to me. My childhood was practically solitary confinement compared to what you're describing."

Alicia was surprised by the note of regret in his voice and looked speculatively at the formidable planes of his face and the aura of power and command that surrounded him. It was hard for her to imagine him as a lonely child.

"There was plenty of companionship, but I always felt that I could never quite measure up." She was silent for a moment as she paused to consider how to explain how inadequate she had felt at times without betraying any crucial weakness to the man opposite her.

"And, of course, I never did measure up. There I was, struggling to top five feet while the boys were walking skyscrapers by the time they hit their teens."

She gave a gurgle of laughter at the memory and reached for her glass of wine. O'Rourke stared at her in fascination. He had never seen her so relaxed. She almost glowed with warmth and vitality, and he felt a deep-seated need to reach out and capture some of it as he would a firefly.

He grasped his own wineglass firmly and remarked encouragingly, "It sounds like quite a tribe. I think I'd like to meet those brothers of yours sometime."

Alicia could almost hear the smile in his voice and could see the warmth in his eyes. The man was trying to charm her again and had halfway succeeded. He was far too easy to like when he was being sensitive and understanding. But she didn't want to be charmed.

"I doubt that you'd have anything in common besides your height...and your domineering attitude toward women," she remarked coldly.

O'Rourke regarded her steadily and refused to be routed by her blatant rudeness. "Were your brothers domineering?"

"Oh, yes," she replied lightly. "My mother died when I was ten, so they had the excuse of looking out for me. It was actually the condescension that bothered me more, as if anything I accomplished could only be the result of their patient and persistent coaching."

"It sounds as if you were very precious to them, that they loved you very much."

Her reply was almost in a monotone and in startling contrast to her previously animated voice. "Yes, but love isn't a license to hold others in stasis, frozen forever like some prehistoric insect in amber."

When she realized what she had said, Alicia felt her hands tremble. Damn O'Rourke for getting past her guard so efficiently. She had never talked to anyone about the way she felt about love.

She clenched her fists in frustration and stared at the food in front of her. Then she straightened her back and looked into O'Rourke's face. "And what about you, Mr. O'Rourke? What's the tale of your young life?"

He knew instinctively that he had somehow come near a nerve, and he felt frustration knot his stomach. Every time he tried to get closer to her she seemed to back farther away. He didn't know how much longer he would be able to take her constant retreating. It wasn't a reaction he was accustomed to from women. For now, though, she was setting the pace, and he would just have to accept it.

"It was pretty ordinary," he said, ignoring her antagonism. "My father was an investment broker in New York and my mother was a lawyer. I was an only child, as you guessed, and I was trained from an early age to follow in my father's footsteps."

It didn't sound a bit ordinary to Alicia. It sounded high-powered and very upper crust. Perhaps he had been a lonely child, she conceded.

"How did you end up owning a winery on the West Coast?" She couldn't resist the promptings of her curiosity.

"After fifteen years on Wall Street, I thought it was time for a breath of fresh air. I had always stayed in touch with Paul, and he's the one who talked me into making an offer for Pheasant Run when it came on the market."

Alicia felt herself beginning to relax again. "Shuffling stock certificates doesn't seem to be a very appropriate apprenticeship for a serious winemaker," she threw at him.

O'Rourke's face darkened, but that was the only indication that her barb had disturbed him. "I never intended to stomp the grapes with my own feet, Alicia. I pay an excellent winemaker an excellent salary to oversee the production of Pheasant Run wines. Nevertheless, I intend to be active in all facets of the business, and I'm not adverse to learning new skills."

Alicia felt rather ashamed of her remark and then decided it was just as well she had insulted him. At least it would make him keep his distance. The thought was oddly disquieting, and she turned her attention back to her plate. The remaining halibut was cold, and the sauce had congealed unappetizingly. She poked at it with her fork and wished the evening was finished.

O'Rourke pushed his plate back and reached for his wine in desperation. He felt like an addict going through withdrawal. His single-minded craving for her dominated him both physically and mentally. It was a relief when Paul approached the table and invited them back to the kitchen.

A sleepy-looking woman sat relaxing at a table against one wall. She waved fondly at them as they entered the bustling room, seemingly unaffected by all the activity, and laconically invited them to join her at the table. "Sit down, sit down. You exhaust me by standing there."

Alicia complied as Connan dropped a friendly kiss on the woman's neatly braided hair.

"Joan, I'd like you to meet a newly converted fan—this is Alicia. She runs the Panache Pantry out at Pheasant Run."

Joan looked at her with interest. "Of course, you do the truffles, don't you?"

Alicia was flattered that she had come to the attention of this talented chef. She laughed and replied, "Chocolate is my secret passion, but I think I've just developed another one. The dressing on your spinach salad will haunt my dreams for months."

The other woman was smiling easily at her, pleased at the genuine note of admiration in her voice. "That's a lovely compliment. Let's all have some coffee and cognac. The best part of this job is that I get to relax after the meals are all cooked and let someone else worry about cleaning up."

Paul and O'Rourke sat down at the table, and in a few moments a waiter delivered steaming coffee and snifters of amber brandy on a tray. The heady aromas were almost a dessert by themselves, and Alicia's entire face was concentrated in appreciation.

"A sensualist." At Joan's emphatic statement she jerked her attention back to her companions to find them all regarding her with amusement.

"You'd better hang on to her," Paul said, teasing O'Rourke with a knowing gleam in his eye. "They're an endangered species, and I've got the only other one in town on contract." His eyes swung affectionately toward Joan, and she gave him a slow, warm smile in return. Alicia flushed when she saw O'Rourke's speculative glance. He was watching her reaction with interest, an unreadable message in his eyes. He turned back to the other couple and drawled, "I'm doing my best, but she seems unreasonably skittish."

"Obviously you have no finesse," retorted Joan. "You look like a cross giant."

Alicia laughed with delight at the unexpected support. "That's exactly what I thought when I first met him. In fact, I still think of him as Goliath."

The Morgans broke into appreciative laughter, and O'Rourke looked distinctly uncomfortable. He hadn't intended Alicia to see him as some kind of threatening monster. A nerve twitched in his jaw and he glanced at her with frustration as she casually ignored him and chatted with Joan.

"The emphasis on regionally produced, locally grown foods is strong back East, of course, but it's just becoming respectable on the West Coast. I think you're going in the right direction with the Panache Pantry," Joan said.

"Sometimes it's like a treasure hunt. I'll hear about someone who's doing something different and then track them down. I spent a whole day once trying to find an old German farmer who was supposed to smoke trout and prime rib."

"Did you find him?"

"I did, but his product turned out to be a close relative of beef jerky and I couldn't use it."

"It sounds like a time-consuming treasure hunt."

"It often is," Alicia said reflectively, "but it's worth it when I find someone like Mary Alice Brannish, who makes the most exquisite goat cheese you've ever tasted."

Connan maintained a semblance of a conversation with Paul, but his attention strayed repeatedly to Alicia. He had never seen her so animated, and it made her attraction even more compelling. He almost groaned at the thought of the distance she had put between them. Why did he have to want her so much that it was an ache? Why did she have to be a tenant in his arcade?

"I think it's time we were on our way," he interrupted. "Alicia's a working woman and has to get up early."

Alicia stood up reluctantly and shook hands with Joan and Paul and allowed Connan to escort her into the hall where they collected her coat. Paul saw them to the door and pressed a slip of paper into her hand, saying, "From Joan."

As they stepped into the bracing night air, she glanced down at the scrap and realized that it was the recipe for the raspberry vinaigrette. Joan's generosity was overwhelming. Most professional chefs guarded their secrets jealously, or sold them for astronomical sums to corporations for mass production.

"Look. She's given me directions for the dressing."

Alicia's hand was clutching at his sleeve in her excitement, and he found the sensation distinctly disturbing. He covered her hand with his own and pressed it harder against his arm as he smiled down at her enthusiasm.

"Joan is a special person. You should be flattered. I don't think that she shares her secrets often."

He led the way to the parked car, and soon they were on their way, Alicia still enveloped in a pleasant glow compounded of equal parts of cognac and the warm reflection of Joan's generosity. As they pulled into the parking garage of her apartment building, panic hit her with unsuspected force. O'Rourke parked the Porsche and turned to face her, looking every inch the predator.

Her words tumbled out in an idiotic babble as she fumbled for the door. "Thank you for dinner. I enjoyed meeting the Morgans. You don't need to come up."

"Don't be ridiculous. I'll see you to your door." His voice was dangerously soft, and he was already out of the car before she could argue. She sighed fatalistically as they walked in silence to the elevators. He still hadn't spoken as the doors opened onto the third floor, and the silence by then was an almost tangible presence thickening the air between them.

Alicia felt the breath catch in her throat as they approached her door. All the conflicting emotions she had tried to suppress boiled dangerously close to the surface, and she knew that she wouldn't be able to avoid facing them much longer.

He made her feel so volatile, as if she might burst into flames at any moment and be consumed. The thought excited and frightened her at the same time. She was drawn toward the flickering heat of his gaze, which seemed to promise so much.

But was it a promise or a demand? She didn't know and wasn't at all sure that she wanted to find out. For years her life had been dominated by big, overwhelming, demanding men just like Connan.

First it had been her older brothers who had pushed and bullied her in the direction they thought she should go. Their brand of overprotective love had sapped her self-confidence and almost smothered her. Then Peter had come along....

Unsteadily she unlocked the door and half turned. "Good night," she muttered, not daring to look at him, not daring to reveal the depth of her confusion and doubt. And while she stood staring dumbly at the floor, he put her gently aside and walked into her apartment.

"Alicia," he said persuasively, "why don't you come in and get comfortable? We still haven't had that talk, and it may take a while."

The rough timbre of his voice started a shiver at the nape of her neck, and she flushed. It was impossible to deny the power of his attraction and the vulnerability she felt because of it.

She stared defiantly at him for several seconds, irritated by his confidence and the easy smile that seemed to say he was in total command of the situation. Once she had been attracted by that same air of supreme confidence and superiority in Peter. But that relationship had taught her to regard big, dominating men as a threat to her autonomy as a person.

Alicia marched through the door and shut it sharply. She hung her coat in the closet and walked toward an old oak rocking chair that sat in an isolated corner of the room. She had promised to listen to him, but she wouldn't be overwhelmed, nor would she be intimidated.

He looked very stern as he stood there in the middle of the room. Suddenly the space was much too small for the two of them, and she shifted uneasily in the chair as she waited for him to begin. He turned abruptly and walked toward the window, his back ramrod straight. When he finally turned to face her, she was shocked at the sharp angularity of his face. He looked like a stranger.

"Alicia, I was totally out of line last night and said some unforgivable things. Hell, I don't know what got into me. I didn't even recognize myself. I lost control, and that's never happened before."

He began pacing again and then stopped in front of her, pinning her to the chair with his look of brooding sensuality. "I don't know what it is between us," he continued hesitantly, "but I know that I like it and I want to explore it. For God's sake, woman, all I can think about is the feel of you in my arms, the taste and smell of you."

His voice was harsh, and he was staring at her intensely. Her body was on fire in response to the mental images he was conjuring up with his words. Her own memory was graphically detailed with textures and sensations of a physical longing that left her trembling.

"I've never been so obsessed in my life, and I feel like I'm out of control. The only thing I know is that—" his voice trailed off and his eyes glittered "—you're mine, Alicia, and even though you're too stubborn to admit it yet, you want me, too. I'll never let you go."

Somehow he had snared her in a net of sexual attraction. Her body sang for him as her mind fought furiously to restrain it.

"It's not true. I don't want you. I don't." Her whispered protest slid up a half tone to become a wondering question, and she realized that, despite all her confusion and doubts about her relationship with Connan, the fact remained that she wanted him very much.

"You want me and I can prove it." His voice was both a challenge and a caress.

As he moved purposefully across the room, Alicia sat frozen, unable to even look away. Dropping a light kiss on the top of her head, he scooped her out of her chair and held her against his chest before lowering his lips to meet hers.

That first contact was seductively gentle as he brushed her mouth with elusive flame. His lips traveled across her face and under the curve of her jaw until they met the smooth, delicate skin of her neck, and Alicia began to tremble. Her guard was crumbling, her resistance drifting away like mist. It had only taken minutes for him to call her desire out of its hiding place, and she moaned softly. Her hands rested at his throat, and she could feel the strong, steady pulse that leaped beneath her fingers. It felt so good to be close to him, enfolded in his gentle strength.

There was wonder and bright passion in his expression as he looked into her eyes. He felt as if he were drowning in a deep pool of serene green water. A small smile tilted the corners of her lips as he gathered her even closer and sank down into the rocker. He bent his head, and she gave him her lips without restraint in a piercingly sweet kiss that shook him to the marrow.

His hands feathered over her, tracing the slope of a shoulder, the full swell of a breast as he memorized the finely drawn outline of her body in a prelude to more intimate explorations. He pushed up the hem of her dress and slid his hand along her thigh, smoothing the sensitive flesh and then withdrawing. Cupping her breast, he found the hard, aroused nipple under the layers of angora, and he groaned. "You've got too much on. I've got to touch you. I've got to feel your soft, smooth body against me."

With an economical movement, he unzipped the back of her dress and pulled it slowly off her shoulders and arms. Holding her close, he breathed the intoxicating scent that clung to her soft skin. His hands

smoothed her shoulders and her back and then
spanned the curve of her waist.

Alicia held her breath in anticipation as his head
bent to hers and he pressed his lips to her temple. He
stayed that way, unmoving for a moment, and she
clutched at his shoulders. His lips began a sensual
journey along the arch of her cheekbone, biting softly,
licking, filling his mouth with her taste and texture,
until he arrived at her lips once more.

At first his kiss was as insubstantial as the gauzy
brush of a dragonfly's wings, a whisper of warmth, a
fleeting sensation that made her long for more. Alicia
tried to press herself more firmly against him, but his
purpose was as inflexible as the arms that controlled
the space of their bodies' intimacy. His lips felt hot
against her own. Teasing with the increased pressure
that she craved, they seared and then withdrew, feeding the fever raged through her body. She had never
felt so intensely about another man before. Peter had
never aroused such emotions, such deep insatiable
longings in her. She felt an overpowering need to touch
Connan, to convince herself that this was more than
a dream.

She fumbled uncertainly at the buttons of his shirt,
and he raised his head to look into her eyes. "Do you
want to touch me, Alicia?" he asked softly, and suddenly it was what she wanted to do more than anything else. Hot blood rushed to her cheeks, but she
couldn't tell him anything less than the truth. Slowly
she nodded. His lips twisted the sound that should
have been a laugh of triumph, and it came out sounding more like a groan.

Holding her firmly in the circle of one arm, he used
his free hand to undo the buttons of his shirt. When it

hung loose and open, he gathered both her hands in his and pressed them against the hard warmth of his chest. She could feel the springy dark hair that curled against her palms, and tentatively she moved her hands over his sculpted masculine contours. Growing bolder, she slipped one hand up to the smooth skin of his shoulder and measured the sleek swell of muscle that seemed to tense and shudder under her delicate fingers.

Irresistibly she was drawn to lay her cheek against his bare skin, but it wasn't enough to still the mysterious clamoring of her senses. With an instinct she didn't know she possessed, she turned her lips against the intriguing texture of his chest and gave a faint sigh of relief. This was what she had been seeking unknowingly: the sweet abrasion of his hard body against her softer one, the salty-sweet taste of him on her lips.

A deep rumble in Connan's chest made her pause and look up into his face. The expression there was set and grim, almost angry. Uncertainty blurred the edge of her longing, and a sudden dismay skittered along the edges of her mind. What was happening to her?

Connan stared into her bewildered eyes for an interminable moment, and then his mouth softened. He smiled at her with such tenderness that she had to bury her face against his chest once more. He held her pressed against him very gently, but she could still feel the steeled tenseness of his body. Then silently he smoothed her dress back over her body and pulled the zipper up to the neck with a curiously impersonal gesture. With one arm around her waist, he settled her close against his side.

The sound of her breathing was labored, and she didn't dare look at the man beside her. She didn't dare betray the surprising emotion that had welled up in her heart so unexpectedly. It had been as if she had found a missing part of herself that she hadn't even known she lacked. She had fought so hard, violently even, against the attraction between them, but the message her heart sang could no longer be denied. Could it be that she was falling in love with Connan O'Rourke?

Chapter Seven

Look at me, Alicia," Connan's voice commanded. "I want to see your eyes." Alicia continued to stare at her fingers, which she knotted in her lap. The wild emotions he inspired in her were frightening. She didn't want to feel that way about anyone, especially Connan O'Rourke. He was too strong. It was suicide to trust her emotions to a man like him. She felt the brush of his fingers against her jaw and sensed the restrained strength in them as they tilted her unwilling face up to his.

"You're so beautiful. Do you have any idea of what you do to me?" She shook her head mutely. She knew what *he* did to *her*. He made her body sing and ache at the same time.

"You make me almost hurt with wanting you. When I saw Richard touching you, I wanted to hit him so hard he'd never get up off the floor."

She was fiercely glad to hear of his jealousy. Somehow it lessened her own vulnerability to him. She risked a glance at his face and then looked quickly away from the blazing passion that she saw there.

"Don't be afraid of me, Alicia. Don't ever be afraid. I know that I seem to lose control when we're together, but this time I'm going to do it right. We're going to talk, and I'm going to make you understand how I feel. A night or a weekend with you isn't enough. I want you more than I've ever wanted any woman in my life. I want to wake up in the morning with you at my side. I want to sleep with you wrapped in my arms every night. I want you totally and absolutely every minute of every day. Nothing less would be enough."

Alicia rocked in the waves of his emotion. She suddenly felt fragile and unsure of herself. Connan's passion both thrilled and dismayed her with its single-minded intensity. His words found an echo in her own thoughts, and she realized that she felt the same way about him. The unwelcome realization brought her no joy, however, merely a sense of dismay. He was trying to push her, manipulate her into a relationship she wasn't sure she wanted. Would the price of getting involved with him be more than she could pay?

Her heart gave an irregular skip, and for a brief instant she felt a ridiculous compulsion to run. She wished desperately that time and events would slow to a more manageable pace. No matter how much they were drawn toward each other, the arcade would still be between them. Wanting him hadn't changed anything essential about who she was or what she wanted; it just added another dimension to her life. Panache Pantry was still there, just as important to her now as it ever was, and she was just as committed to her plans for expansion.

"Connan," she whispered, and her voice betrayed her turmoil. "You're going much too fast. I can't deny that there is a strong attraction between us...that I find you attractive..." Her voice trailed off as his arm tightened around her shoulders.

"Attraction? What a pale word, Alicia," Connan said close to her ear. His warm breath feathered her skin like a delicate caress. "You want me just as I want you. Say it, Alicia. I want to hear the words on your lips."

Already troubled by his possessiveness, his insistence on this small capitulation made her stiffen. Then she became aware of his thumb massaging the fine line of her collarbone through the angora dress, and she was overwhelmed once again by the delightful sensations he called to life in her body. She let herself relax against him and sighed. "Yes, I want you."

"You might try to sound more enthusiastic about the idea," he said with a laugh.

Alicia's smile touched the corners of her mouth but didn't reach her eyes. "I'm not sure that I can. The situation is impossible and you know it. I've always thought that loving one's enemies is best done from a safe distance."

The humor faded from his eyes and was replaced by a look of fierce determination. "I've never thought of you as an enemy, Alicia. From the first I've been aware of something special between the two of us. It took me a while to figure it out. I'm not usually so slow on the uptake, but I guess I can blame it on my lack of experience."

"Lack of experience?" Alicia's voice was incredulous.

"Yes, lack of experience," he repeated firmly. "Not that I pretend to have led the life of a monk. There have been women in my life, but things have always been casual and uncommitted for all parties concerned. I've never wanted anything more than that until you came storming into my life. So you see, wrestling with the idea of something like commitment has been a new experience for me."

He smiled a big, confident smile that warmed Alicia with hope. Perhaps she had been unduly pessimistic. Suddenly she wanted to hope. Desperately she wanted to believe that they could work things out and come to some kind of a compromise about the arcade and shop that would satisfy them both and allow them to come together unhampered by conflict or lack of honesty. She would have to tell him about the tenants' organization, but he would understand why she had done it. He knew how important the Panache Pantry was to her. She smiled at him. "Connan, about the Pantry."

"I know, darling," he interrupted gently. "The arcade and the Pantry pose a bit of a problem. You're so involved, you devote so much of your time to your business, that trying to juggle our schedules would be a real nightmare. God, we'd be lucky to see each other a couple of times a week. I don't think that would be enough for either one of us. And, to be frank, the thought of love by appointment leaves me cold."

Alicia's forehead wrinkled as she tried to follow his train of thought. "A bit of a problem" seemed to understate the difficulties, but he was right about their schedules. They would have to budget their time, but she was convinced it would be worth it. She frowned again. He seemed to be missing the point: their opposing stances on the question of her lease at the arcade.

He looked at her warmly and reached over to tuck a stray curl behind her ear. "The problems evaporate, though, as soon as we can get the arcade phased out." He pulled her into his embrace, oblivious to the stiffening of her body, and rubbed his chin against her hair. "I want you in my arms at the end of the day, Alicia, not chasing off with a tray of stuffed mushrooms to some god-awful wedding reception."

As if she could elude the sense of his words by not moving, Alicia sat very still. She felt a withering inside her and knew that she hadn't mistaken his meaning. He didn't understand about the Pantry at all, or didn't care. He thought it all some kind of joke. His apparent sensitivity extended only as far as his own hungers and needs. He hadn't given hers a thought.

He cupped her chin with one big hand and continued in a voice that was rough with sensuality. "You won't have to worry about being bored. I've already thought of several ways to keep you delightfully busy."

Alicia jerked away from him so furiously that she almost fell to the floor.

"Go to the devil, O'Rourke, and find someone else to keep delightfully busy." She looked at his shocked face and laughed bitterly. "You look surprised. What's wrong? Did you think your well-practiced technique was infallible? This may come as a surprise, but it would take a lot more than what you're offering to make me give up the Pantry."

"Alicia, don't. You've got it all wrong." His face was incredulous as he reached out to touch her.

She slipped away and looked at him with loathing from across the room. "Is that what they call a sweet deal in your circles—a bed partner and the arcade all wrapped up in one neat package? I'm afraid I have to disappoint you. The honor of sharing your bed doesn't tempt me to give up everything I've slaved for these past three years. You're good, O'Rourke, but you know that already, don't you? Well, I'm not in the market for any more rehearsed seductions, so you can just save it for someone else."

"What are you talking about?" Connan roared at her as his bewilderment was replaced by anger.

Frigidly she turned her back on him. "Get out," she spat over her shoulder.

He was at her side in a second, spinning her around to face him so that he could stop her hate-filled words with his hard mouth.

She moaned, and the sound was a mixture of arousal and despair. Her body leaped to his touch with an eagerness that was impossible to check. Connan tilted her face so he could look into her eyes. "You see how it is between us? How can you call this rehearsed?" He brushed his thumb over her kiss-swollen lips. "Listen to me," he continued persuasively. "Maybe I misunderstood or assumed too much, but we have too much to give it all up now. We can work something out."

She pulled away, and he let his arm drop, his eyes never leaving her face.

"You haven't proven anything," she said dully as her anger cooled and was replaced by despair, "except that I'm a fool. You've dismissed my work as a childish triviality and you've played with me like a toy. I'll never forgive you for that. You've taken everything from me, including my self respect.''

She looked blindly at him, numb with shock as she fought against her own vulnerability to him.

Connan's face was frozen into a mask of stretched skin and jutting bone. He reached a big hand toward her and smoothed her tumbled hair with a strangely gentle motion. When she flinched from his touch, his eyes darkened to a bleak and barren gray. His voice was harsh when he spoke but coldly controlled and filled with implacable purpose.

''For an intelligent woman you're incredibly blind, Alicia. You have some emotional attachment to the arcade and everything connected to it. You refuse to face the fact that the arcade is not working. I've never come across a less suitable location for a business like yours, and it's a miracle that you've lasted as long as you have.''

His tone moderated, and he continued in a deceptively gentle voice, ''You're out of control and obviously incapable of listening to reason, but don't think this is finished. I'm flying to New York tomorrow afternoon and will be gone for a week. That should give you time to settle down. When I get back we'll talk again.''

From a long way away she registered the sound of the door closing. Standing frozen in the middle of the room, she repeated over and over, ''I won't break down, I won't break down.'' The tears threatened to brim over, but they subsided, leaving her eyes hot and dry and aching. She moved to the window and stood staring out at the night.

How could she have fallen in love with him? How could she have forgotten the pain she'd experienced after her relationship with Peter had disintegrated? Connan's parting words had cut her to the quick. She tried to block out the image of his commanding height and broad shoulders but found that he had cast his shadow into every corner of her mind. I'll get over it, she told herself fiercely. It'll just take time. And bleakly she contemplated the hours and days that stretched before her, barren as a great desert.

"Did you get run over by a truck or something? You look half dead," Richard said the next morning, looking her over critically and noting her puffy eyes and woebegone expression.

She smiled grimly at his greeting. "It's an optical illusion. I'm just fine."

"If you say so," he said doubtfully. "Greenway Tours just called. They had to rearrange their itinerary and want to know if we can come up with thirty box lunches by 1:00. Their group is touring the winery at 2:00."

Gratitude washed through her like a warm tide. The rush order would keep her fully occupied for the morning without any time left over to brood or feel sorry for herself. That was the cure, she decided, just as it had been when Peter had walked out of her life. She would dedicate herself to the Panache Pantry. She would let it absorb every ounce of her energy, both physical and mental. In time Connan would fade from her thoughts and she would heal.

She turned to the phone decisively. "I'll call them and say we accept. How are our supplies, by the way?"

"Aren't you supposed to ask that first?" he teased gently. "No problem. We can manage."

Alicia confirmed the order and then went to work cutting fruit and filling cartons with salad. Richard assembled boxes and carved a smoked turkey for sandwiches. By noon the last napkin was tucked into the last box and they were finished.

"Whew. We ought to get double time for that. You're really in high gear today." Richard mopped his forehead with a napkin.

"Do you want a cup of coffee?" Alicia asked as she poured one for herself.

"No thanks. I'll stick to water. You drink too much of that stuff, you know. It'll make your hair fall out."

Alicia shoved the untidy mass back from her face, impatient with herself for remembering Connan's fascination with it. "Good," she said sharply. "There's way too much of it. Have you had time to look over the menu for the bank party?"

"Sure, boss, and I think we ought to give them the prawn and chutney canapés I was talking about. Early this morning I whipped up a few, and they're fantastic."

"Convince me."

Richard went to the walk-in and removed a small tray of garnished tidbits. Each small square of thinly sliced brown bread had been buttered and then layered with finely chopped chutney, a split prawn and a light sprinkling of paper-thin slices of scallion.

"They certainly look edible," she teased as she took a bite. "Mmm. Richard, I'm surprised. These are almost as good as my favorite sweet and sour."

"Sweet and sour! You've got to be kidding. That's my very own green pear chutney with subtle overtones of ginger and a little hot chili pepper. You are nothing but a Philistine, my dear," he told her loftily. "The Cantonese school of Chinese cooking caters to only the most insipid of palates."

"Richard, you maniac, you've done it again. They're marvelous." She gave him an affectionate pat on the shoulder and reached for another canapé. "Go ahead and put them on the menu. Any other suggestions?"

"No, I'd say it looks pretty good. I thought I'd do a dolphin for the ice carving. Isn't that the bank's logo?"

"Yes. That would be perfect. We'll have them groveling at our feet to do their holiday catering. By December the lines will be out the door and down the street."

"Well, they would be if we had a street," Richard said, his voice casually cynical.

Hearing an unusual note of dissatisfaction in his voice, Alicia looked at him sharply. "Now just what do you mean by that?"

Richard flushed but looked stubborn. "What I mean is, with your head and my hands we ought to be doing a lot better than we are."

Alicia smiled in relief, glad that nothing more serious was bothering him. "You're just impatient, Richard. It's going to take time, but you'll see those lines yet."

"It's going to take more than time. It's going to take a decent location, some place in the center of things, not this cutesy little place stuck out in the middle of nowhere."

"Cutesy little place!" Alicia was outraged.

He slanted her a crooked grin. "Okay, I take back the cutesy, but you have to admit we're stuck in the middle of nowhere."

"I don't admit anything," she said obstinately. "This place has almost more activity than we can handle in the summertime."

"That's only three short months, Alicia. The rest of the time we're stagnant. How many more mossy winters are you going to be able to take before you go completely around the bend?"

"It's not that bad," she said slowly, almost pleadingly.

Richard sensed his advantage and pressed it. "I never have understood your attachment to this place. It's too small, there's not enough traffic year round and the location is inconvenient."

Alicia felt her stomach lurch, and all the bleakness she had been holding at bay rushed forward to overwhelm her.

"The size is a problem," she admitted, uneasily remembering Connan's accusations about her blindness over the arcade.

"And not the only one," he insisted.

She paused and looked at him searchingly. "You're right about the weakness of the arcade, but no site is going to be perfect. At least here we know what the negatives are. If we relocated, we'd have to repeat the whole process of trial and error." He didn't say anything, so she tried to instill a little more confidence into her voice. "I think the arcade has a lot more potential than anyone gives it credit for. The facility is absolutely unique. There isn't another genuine imitation château for miles around."

Richard obliged with a smile and then ruined the effect by replying succinctly, "No guts, no glory."

"You sound just like O'Rourke," she said crossly.

"O'Rourke?" Richard seemed surprised, but an expression of amused comprehension settled across his face almost immediately. "Suddenly I see a thread of method meandering through your madness. Godzilla wants you to relocate, doesn't he?"

Alicia shrugged her shoulders. It wasn't the moment she would have chosen to tell Richard about the arcade, but since he had half guessed anyway she couldn't see a way around it.

"That's part of it," she admitted. "But his first priority is to phase out all the shops and get rid of the arcade entirely. He's even offered to buy out the remaining time on my lease to expedite the process."

Richard whistled admiringly. "Now that's what I call fast work. He's only been here a week, and it's taken me a whole year to figure it out. Where are you going to go?"

"Nowhere," she retorted sharply. "Like I said, I think the arcade has untapped potential, and I'm not about to call it quits." Her eyes hardened uncharacteristically as she thought of O'Rourke and his self-serving manipulations. "Everything else aside, I don't like being pushed. I'm going to make a lot of noise and put up a fight O'Rourke will never forget. That's what Martha and I have been working on this past week. We're trying to organize a tenants' rights group to protect all of our interests."

"That'll throw some dust in his eyes, all right," Richard said with amusement.

She felt a slight flush begin to glow across her cheekbones. He had unerringly recognized the vengeful note in her voice, and for a moment she felt embarrassed. Then she hardened herself against any regrets. She didn't care if her motives weren't the purest. O'Rourke deserved everything he got, and she refused to have any misplaced scruples about it.

"That's the idea," she admitted honestly. "In fact, I'd better touch base with Martha right now."

As she walked the short distance to Martha's shop, she could hear the unmistakable sound of angry voices. Martha was giving some poor soul the sharp edge of her tongue, and Alicia wondered who had the temerity to get her so angry. When she walked through the door she couldn't see anyone, but she could hear the strident tones of Martha's voice rising from the stockroom. "I won't do it, you walking earthquake, so don't try your tricks on me. You're in quicksand, and you'd better start shoveling."

She erupted into the shop and pulled up short when she saw Alicia.

"Martha, what's going on? It sounds like a dogfight in here." Alicia's voice trailed off to a whisper as Connan stepped out of the stockroom. It was obvious that he was furious about something, and she felt her precariously balanced equilibrium totter. Her face went white, and she wondered how long it would take to tame the leaping impulse that urged her to throw herself into his arms, to accept whatever he offered.

He strode to her side and captured one of her hands, his long brown fingers smoothing over the frantic pulse in her wrist. Totally ignoring Martha's presence, he spoke in a deep, compelling voice. "Did you come to see me off, Alicia? Don't do anything irrevocable while I'm gone.'' Then he pressed a slow, melting kiss to her lips and left.

Alicia balled her fists and stared furiously at his retreating back. If there had been something big and rotten at hand, she would have thrown it at him.

"Pretty hot stuff,'' Martha said mischievously. "Does this mean the resistance movement is off?''

Alicia unclenched her fists and took a deep breath before turning to face Martha's curiosity. "Of course not. I'm more determined than ever to pull it off. Connan O'Rourke is a selfish, egotistical bully, and it's time somebody stood up to him.''

"Is that what we're doing?'' Martha asked mildly. "I thought we were trying to save the shops.''

"That, too,'' Alicia snapped impatiently. "But it's the principle of the thing. I've had firsthand experience with his kind. He's totally self-centered, completely amoral and ruthless. He'll stoop to anything to get what he wants, no matter who gets hurt.'' Her voice trailed off and then came back stronger than ever.

"He wants the arcade cleared out and he wants me—at least until someone more attractive comes along.'' She looked around Martha's pleasantly cluttered shop, her eyes skimming the baskets of bright wool and the stacks of heather-colored sweaters.

"Is that right?'' Martha asked thoughtfully. "I take it you turned him down.''

"Of course I turned him down.'' Alicia's voice was flat as her anger ebbed. "I may be the biggest fool that ever walked the face of the earth, but I'm not stupid. I can still recognize a sleazy bargain when I see one.''

Pain twisted momentarily in the wake of her anger, but she ruthlessly beat it back. Connan O'Rourke wasn't worth a single regret. He had almost fooled her with his talk of commitment, with his hungry kisses and hot, gentle hands that had made her forget the past and Peter's harsh betrayal.

"Alicia?" Martha's anxious voice broke into her bitter thoughts.

"Sorry, Martha. I didn't mean to unload it all on you."

"What are friends for? We are friends, aren't we?" Martha seemed anxious for reassurance.

Alicia patted her hand and smiled. "Of course we are, even if you do fraternize with the enemy." A teasing note came into her voice. "What was going on when I came in? O'Rourke certainly has a talent for making people lose their tempers. It sounded like you were chewing his ears off."

Martha's face furrowed, and she avoided Alicia's eyes. "I was hoping you wouldn't ask," she muttered, "but it was bound to come out sooner or later."

"What on earth are you talking about?" Alicia demanded, halfway between amusement and impatience.

"I'm talking about Connan. We're sort of connections."

"Connections?" Alicia parroted blankly.

"Yes, you know, like relatives."

Alicia scrambled to make sense of her words. Martha looked at her expectantly, and she had to bite back the laughter that threatened to overwhelm her. Martha was a master at deadpan deliveries. "You've got to be kidding," she finally choked out. "Next you'll be telling me you're his mother."

Martha looked as if she had been insulted. "No such thing," she said tartly. "But I am his great-aunt for all my sins."

"You're not joking, are you?" Alicia asked quietly. Her thoughts were racing. Martha had always been her confidante and lately her ally as well. It didn't make any sense to her at all, and she pushed her hair back from her face with a hunted gesture. It was beginning to look as if Alicia Stevenson had been born to be the world's fool. She hadn't enough sense to pick her friends wisely, let alone a lover.

"You don't see me laughing, do you, Red?" Martha's voice was gentle but determined. "You see, I was having a little trouble with my blood pressure, and my doctor said I had to back off some, not work so much. Well, that was easier said than done. I'd had my shop in Seattle for twenty years and was well established. It was a busy place in a shopping mall, and I had classes six nights a week. Anyway, Connan took a flying trip up to see me and sort of took over. He found a buyer for the shop, moved me down here and set me up in the arcade.

"He guaranteed the pace would be slow, with just enough business to keep me interested and not kill me. When I first saw this place, I thought I would die from boredom. It was the exact opposite of my other place—miles from anywhere and no reason on earth for anyone to make the trip if they weren't interested in wine. In fact, if I hadn't been semiretired I wouldn't have even considered it. But once I got used to the change, I enjoyed it—almost like a vacation. It might not be much of a place to start a business, but it's a perfect place to retire."

Alicia met Martha's direct gaze and nodded. "Despite opinions to the contrary, I'm not blind or stupid. I get the point. Did Connan ask you to do his dirty work for him?"

"He did not, and even if he did I wouldn't have." Martha was righteously indignant.

"I suppose not," Alicia agreed. "He's more than capable of doing it all by himself." Her thoughts had the distinct bitterness of gall. The past twenty-four hours had certainly ripped away any remaining illusions she might have had concerning the arcade. Connan, Richard and Martha made a formidable commando force that even her stubbornness couldn't withstand. She looked at Martha with faint curiosity. "If you were so convinced that the arcade is a dead end, why did you bother to get involved in the tenants' organization with me?"

Alicia was surprised to see the flush that spread over the older woman's weathered cheekbones. "Well, things were kind of slow after the summer, and I liked your spunk, and, well...I guess I was bored," she ended on a note of defiance.

Alicia looked at the chagrined expression on her friend's features and laughed. "Martha, you old devil. Do you mean to tell me that you got involved just for the fun of watching the fur fly?"

Martha was totally unrepentant. "That's about the size of it, I suppose," she admitted. "Connan's a convincing son of a gun, and I knew he'd be able to handle it." She looked slyly at Alicia and added, "Besides, I never could resist the opportunity to play Cupid. I thought if you two were at each other's throats, something interesting might come out of it."

The smile faded from Alicia's lips, and her voice was cold when she replied, ''You're way off base, Martha. The only thing I want from Connan O'Rourke is distance, and plenty of it.''

Chapter Eight

Alicia felt hunted as she moved through the weekend. It was only the sure knowledge that she wouldn't have to face Connan for a week that kept her going. It was painful to admit that he had been right about the arcade, that she had been as blind as he had accused her of being. She wouldn't have believed her own capacity for self-deception if it hadn't been forcibly rammed down her throat.

In retrospect, of course, it was perfectly obvious. She had been hurt and she'd sought a safe place to hide and lick her wounds. Panache Pantry had been her sanctuary, and she had crouched there for almost three years like a quivering rabbit. The image made her cringe with embarrassment. She supposed she ought to be grateful to Connan for bringing the fact to her attention.

Gratitude was the last thing she felt toward Connan O'Rourke, however. His commanding image rose unbidden in her mind, and she was suddenly deluged with remembered sensations—the solid muscular feel of his chest beneath her cheek, the languorous velvet of his lips against her skin, the quickened rasp of his breath in her hair. God, he had made her feel so alive.

It was all counterfeit, she reminded herself as she forced the disturbing memories from her mind. It meant less than nothing. The tender feelings that had been aroused by his practiced caresses were just one more illusion. He was cold and calculating, manipulating people to further his own ends. How could she possibly have been attracted to a man like that?

Ruthlessly she forced the memories aside and turned her thoughts to more productive channels. She was going to have to make some decisions about the shop, she realized. She had finally accepted the fact that the arcade was a dead end, but that didn't mean that the Panache Pantry wasn't still a viable business. Even with the handicap of a poor location, she had managed to build her reputation to a respectable level. She had a lot to be proud of, she reminded herself fiercely, and even the masterful O'Rourke couldn't take that away from her. She was efficient, creative and competitive, and she wasn't interested in being anything else. Connan could go buy himself a poodle if he wanted a bed warmer.

The hurt she wasn't quite ready to admit gave way to the more satisfying emotion of anger. Damn the man for thinking he could walk in and take over her life, for thinking she was a besotted fool who would respond with a simper when he whistled. She'd show him what she was made of.

Peter had wanted to take over every facet of her life as well. Maybe it was in the blood of tall, strong men

to want to smother small, slightly built women. With
Peter she had allowed it to happen, even welcomed his
dictating her life. She'd thought it an expression of his
love. He had chosen the movies they saw, the friends
they'd gone out with, even the frilly dresses he'd
thought suitable for his future wife. He had been so
sophisticated, so attentive, compared to her pack of
rowdy brothers and their boisterous friends, who always treated her like one of the gang.

She had been too inexperienced to recognize when
the attentiveness became control, when the cherishing
became outright manipulation. She had been in love
and willing to sacrifice anything for Peter.

Inexplicably he had become bored with the sub-
dued, acquiescent Alicia he had created and had
walked out of her life one day with scarcely an explanation. She had been so emotionally drained that she
couldn't even hate him, but she had promised herself
fiercely that no man would ever take that much from
her again. She was a person not an accessory. She
might give, but she would not be taken.

Sunday night she found herself wandering aim-
lessly around her apartment. She went into the kitchen
to make some coffee and, halfway through the process, changed her mind and rummaged through the
cupboards for a bottle of wine that had been a birth-
day present from Richard. She poured herself a glass
and carried it back into the living room. She switched
on the stereo and then turned it off again, settling instead for an old movie on television. Cradling the glass
in her hands, she stared at the images of Fred Astaire
and Ginger Rogers swirling across the screen in im-
probable unison.

Connan continued to intrude on her thoughts. How could he expect her to give up everything that made her an individual, to turn her life into a tight little orbit with him at the center? She could never become that kind of a mindless being. She had admitted her attraction to him, but that didn't mean she was suicidal. A relationship with Connan O'Rourke would ultimately be destructive.

She set the untouched glass of wine on a table and got up to turn off the TV. Wandering over to the window, she stared out over the city.

Though there were some loose ends to tie up, she had decided what she had to do. Monday was her day off, and she would make an appointment with a commercial real estate broker first thing in the morning and start looking for a new location. It galled her to present her lease to the mighty O'Rourke on a silver platter. It would have given her a great deal of satisfaction to put up a good fight, but honesty compelled her to admit that it would be a waste of her time and energy. O'Rourke might be an insufferable bully, but in this case he was right about the location.

There were the other tenants to consider as well. It simply wasn't fair to involve them in what amounted to a personal vendetta. They would all be better off in a more suitable location as well, and she owed it to them to explain that.

She wasn't looking forward to the upcoming tenants' meeting. After getting everyone riled up over the situation, she was going to have to explain how she ended up in the opposite camp. It would amount to a public confession of stupidity and was bound to be humiliating. She couldn't see a way around it, however, and only hoped that they would understand without her having to go into too many personal details.

She gritted her teeth. O'Rourke had the nerve to talk about commitment. He didn't know the first thing about the word. Commitment was when you didn't shy away from a task just because it was unpleasant. It was being concerned about something besides your own convenience. It was *giving* once in a while instead of *taking*.

In the morning she leafed through the yellow pages as she ate breakfast and made notes of several possible agents. There was no need to rush on Mondays, so she took a leisurely bath in an effort to relax her tense muscles. After dressing she sat down by the phone and stared at it for several minutes before finally forcing herself to pick up the receiver. She'd made her decision, and it was time to take the first step. The following ones would be easier. Resolutely she dialed the first number on her list and, after a brief conversation, made an appointment with the agent for 11:00.

Methodically she cleaned up the apartment and then stuffed a notebook into her purse before running down the stairs to the garage. Mable's engine coughed into life, and Alicia drove the van with single-minded concentration to the commercial real estate office she had chosen.

Ted Lindberg was sifting through a stack of papers at his desk and rose to greet her as she walked through the door.

"Hi, there. You must be Alicia Stevenson. Take a chair and I'll show you what I've come up with so far. This is a list of all the available sites that fit your general needs in terms of square footage, price range and access. I've included several that are located in shopping malls, although I'm not sure that's what you're after.''

"Actually, I hadn't considered a mall location, and my instinct says no. It might be worth looking at one or two, though. I might change my mind."

"You'll notice that I've starred about a dozen of the listings. Those are ones that I think you might find the most interesting. The descriptions are pretty basic, but they'll give you something to work with. Now, are you sure you don't want me to take you around? I'd be happy to do it. It's all part of the service."

"Thanks for the offer, but I prefer to poke around by myself for now," Alicia said, shaking her head. "I'll call you if I need any additional information."

"That'll be fine. I'm here every day. Even if you don't find exactly what you're looking for on that list, stay in touch. We have new listings coming in every day."

They shook hands, and Alicia walked out, clutching the sheets of paper. She climbed into the van and sat for a moment, staring at the list in her hand. This is my future, she reminded herself. She scanned the first page and noticed that one of the addresses was within a mile of where she sat. She turned Mable in the appropriate direction and drove off to check it out.

"Some future," she muttered in disgust as she surveyed the dingy concrete-block building. It had obviously housed a hamburger stand at one time and the windows were still greasy from the former occupant. It stood by itself at the corner of a busy intersection that no one in his right mind would consider lingering at. She vigorously crossed the address off and got back in the van.

She consulted the list again and found a prospect located in the same general area as her apartment. It took a while to find the spot. The location, tucked into a row of nondescript shops, was on the first floor of a three-story sandstone building, which dated from the turn of the century. There was very little activity in the area, and the prevailing atmosphere was one of decay. She crossed out another address.

Pulling up to a convenience store, she bought herself a carton of yogurt and an apple and then drove to a nearby park to eat her lunch. As she ate, she kept her mind resolutely focused on the logistical problems of relocating. She would have to put together a mailing list of regular customers so that they would know where to find her. New product lines would have to be considered, and she needed to finalize her plans for the Pantry Café.

By the time she had gnawed to the core of her apple, she had begun to build an image of what her new establishment would be like. Bustling, definitely a bustling sort of place with lots of people going in and out, she thought. There would be a bell to add to the busy noise every time someone opened the door. She wondered if she could afford an espresso machine—it would be a great attraction for the early-morning breakfast contingent. She could serve giant cinnamon rolls, hot out of the oven, and the smell alone would draw people from miles around.

The sheaf of papers on the bench beside her rustled with a sudden gust of wind. She grabbed them and raised her eyes to the sky. A heavy bank of dark clouds obscured the sun, and the wind was rising. The temperature had suddenly dropped, and she realized it was getting ready to rain.

Gathering her things together, she walked back to the van, determined to continue her search. The next two places she checked out were absolutely impossible, and the third was a very tentative maybe. It was only the first day, and she was getting discouraged already.

By four o'clock the rain was sheeting the windshield, and all she could think about was a hot cup of coffee. Her shoes were soaked through and her legs splashed with mud. The skies had been clear when she'd left the apartment, so she hadn't bothered with a jacket, and now she was shivering in the damp cold. She had hoped to find something before Connan got back from New York, but at this rate her search could go on for months.

She wanted to have a new lease firmly in hand to wave in Connan's face when she backed down over the arcade. It was important to her that he realize that she was completely capable of taking charge of her own life both personally and professionally without any condescending handouts from him.

Alicia squared her shoulders. Richard would be willing to cover the shop for her while she spent more time looking for a location. In fact, he'd probably push her out into the street when he heard the news. With just a little luck, and a lot of concentrated effort, she'd have a new lease by the end of the week.

She turned on the heat when she got home, stripped off her wet clothing and took a hot shower. The warmth seeped through her body gradually and eased some of her mental tension as well. She still had time, she consoled herself. Connan wouldn't be back before the weekend. That gave her five days to find a new home for the Panache Pantry. She'd talk to

Richard in the morning and ask him to cover for her while she continued the search.

The phone rang as she wrapped a fluffy towel around herself, and she hurried to answer it.

"Hello, Alicia," Connan's voice sounded over the line clearly, and her heart seemed to stop in midbeat.

"Connan, I . . . you . . . Where are you?" It was a stupid question, but the familiar timbre of his voice unnerved her.

"I'm in New York. Where did you expect me to be?"

"In New York, I guess. It's just that your voice is so clear, you could be calling from next door."

"If I was next door, you can bet I wouldn't be calling you on the phone." His voice was mocking.

Alicia wanted to hang up, but her hand wouldn't obey. "What do you want?" Her voice was frozen. She didn't want to talk to him; she didn't even want to think about him.

"You don't sound very pleased to hear from me."

"I'm not," she answered shortly.

His voice dropped an octave and became suddenly husky. "I miss you, and if this is a taste of the future you had in mind, I'm not having any. There's something special between us, and I won't let you throw it away. I know I made a colossal mess of things. I took far too much for granted about you and the Pantry, but, Alicia, I was never using you. Everything between us was real, and you've got to believe that."

She felt battered by his intensity and torn by her own desires. For a brief moment she considered responding to the almost desperate note in his voice. Then her stronger self rejected the thought as a dangerous weakness.

"Your motives don't interest me, and I find your 'wanting' offensive." Strain made her voice harsh.

"What you're really saying is that I can't compete with your business. It's more important to you than anything we might have together." There was no mistaking the bitterness in his voice this time. "I wouldn't have believed you were such a coward, Alicia. Hell, I should have known better than to try to talk to you over the phone. We'll thrash it out when I get back."

The phone clicked abruptly as he hung up, and Alicia was left listening to the empty tone in stunned silence. What was it that made her so unreasonably susceptible to the man? The mere sound of his voice made her heart pound. He continuously breached her defenses, and she discovered a secret part of herself that ached to respond to him. She wouldn't be a victim again, she wouldn't. She was in charge of her life and she couldn't allow him to take her over, no matter how strong the temptation.

The next morning she caught a glimpse of her reflection in the window as she unlocked the door to the shop, and smiled wryly. She was wearing her new challis skirt with the dusty rose sweater. It made her look like a gypsy, carefree and independent. It was an appropriate, if not entirely accurate image. The familiar potpourri of aromas greeted her as she walked through the door, and her stomach did a little flip. She realized that she had missed another dinner and promised herself a good breakfast. Back in the kitchen, she got the coffee going and then turned on the oven to heat up a piece of smoked salmon quiche. Within fifteen minutes she was seated at her desk, looking over the calendar between bites of food. She was so engrossed that she didn't hear Richard come in and was startled by his greeting.

"Morning. Are you going to a carnival later today, or did you just get back from one?"

"Good morning, Richard." She turned in her chair to face him. "You're observant this morning."

"I'd have to be blind to miss that getup. As a matter of fact, my eyes are a little dazzled by the brightness." He squinted at her and then closed his eyes and fumbled his way toward the coffeepot.

Alicia laughed at his clowning. "You're in an awfully good mood this morning. Did you have a nice day off?"

"Fine. I sketched out the dolphin for the ice carving so that I could get started on it today."

"Great. I've never seen an ice carving in progress before, so this should be interesting."

She reached for her coffee and took a sip. "By the way, I looked at some commercial property in downtown Portland yesterday." Her tone was exaggeratedly casual, and she watched Richard's face intently for a reaction.

"You did what?" His voice came out in an excited squeak.

"I didn't see anything really suitable, though." She shrugged dismissively and turned back to her quiche. An explosion of raucous sound jerked her head around again, and she watched with delight as Richard's angular body performed an impromptu war dance in the middle of the kitchen.

When he pulled her out of the chair, she didn't resist, grateful for his exuberant reception of the news. He began to pelt her with questions. "What have you seen so far? Have you been looking in the suburbs or downtown? Some of those new skyscrapers have ritzy little retail spaces. Don't keep me in suspense. Tell me something.'' He ended on a pleading note, and Alicia cuffed his arm playfully.

''Don't worry. I'm not looking at anything cutesy. So far I haven't found the right spot, but I know it's out there just waiting for me to discover it and turn it into a gold mine.''

Richard widened his eyes and chanted fervently, ''I do believe, I do believe.''

''I'm glad to hear it, but do you think you can keep your feet on the ground long enough to take over the shop for the next couple of days while I do some more looking?''

''All this and a promotion, too? I don't know if I can handle it, boss—manager pro tem of the ghost-town pantry?''

''Don't rub it in,'' she advised him. ''I'll finish Mrs. Jorgensen's hors d'oeuvres this morning. She's coming in at three to pick everything up. That'll give you a chance to work on the dolphin. Tomorrow and Thursday I'll spend the day cruising the streets of Portland. Do you think you can manage most of the prep for the bank party on Wednesday? I'll come in at four to do the trays and garnishing.''

''No problem, O Fearless Leader.'' He pulled a pair of yellow earmuffs out of his pocket. ''You may want to make yourself scarce for half an hour while I do the rough work on the ice with my trusty chainsaw.''

Alicia grimaced as he gave her a diabolical grin and revved up the engine. The shriek of the blade hitting the ice was unbearable and she hastily retreated into the shop and shut the connecting door behind her. She wandered over to the window and stood staring at her display. It looked good, and a tiny flicker of pride warmed her. Unconsciously she straightened her shoulders.

A tapping on the window distracted her, and she looked up to see Martha smiling rather tentatively through the glass. She waved for her to come in, and the straight-backed woman stepped through the door.

"What's going on back there? It sounds like you've got a team of demolition experts in the kitchen."

Alicia laughed. "It's just Richard and his trusty chainsaw working on an ice carving. He's creating a dolphin for a retirement party we're catering."

Martha winced as a particularly raucous burst of noise drifted through the closed door. "I can't hear myself think with that unholy racket going on. Listen, something's come up and we need to talk. Grab some coffee and come over to my shop. I'll tell you all about it."

Martha trotted off, and Alicia stared blankly after her. There had been a gleam in the other woman's eyes that did nothing for her peace of mind. With a frustrated sigh, she hurried into the back to let Richard know she was leaving, then poured two mugs of coffee as Martha had commanded.

When Alicia delivered the coffee, Martha was looking very smug as she rocked rather energetically in the back corner of her shop. "Our jeweler got back early, Alicia—and he's very interested." Alicia looked at her blankly.

She'd thought she had more time. Larsen had not been expected back until the end of the week, and she had planned on using those few days to sift through real estate. She wasn't mentally prepared to face the tenants yet.

"How did you find out he was back?" She sank into the other rocker and avoided Martha's sharp glance.

"Well, I had to stop by the shop to pick up a few things yesterday and I ran into him in the hall. He cut his trip short and wanted to get a head start on the week. When I told him what was going on, he blew a fuse. It seems he just plunked down a big check for new inventory, and the thought of being forced out of the arcade made him see red. He got on the phone to his attorney and howled at him for fifteen minutes. I've never seen the old boy so lively." Martha grinned at her expectantly. "It looks like we're going to go into that meeting with all guns blazing. Larsen and Ben can hardly wait to march up to Connan's office and confront him." Martha's enjoyment of the brouhaha was unholy.

"Martha, you're a wicked old woman. After our discussion about the arcade, I didn't expect you to keep on feeding the fires," Alicia said with exasperation.

Martha looked at her innocently. "When you didn't say anything about waving a white flag, I assumed you had decided to let a poor old lady have her fun."

Alicia ignored her plaintive tones. "I've just started looking for a new location, and now I have to face Larsen's irate lawyer on top of a whole pack of howling fellow tenants."

"Just a minute, Red. You've lost me. If you're looking for a new location, what are you bothering about the tenants' organization for?"

"I started it, and I think I have a responsibility to finish it, Martha." Alicia's voice was quiet and very serious. "I made a mistake about the arcade, and I'm willing to admit it, but that doesn't change the fact that I made a commitment to Larsen and Ben and all the others. They were ready to support me, and I owe them honesty if nothing else."

"Hmmph!" Martha snorted. "If Larsen is anything to go by, you may have a little problem in getting them to swallow your honesty."

"I suppose so, but I'm going to give it a try. Have you set a date for the meeting yet?"

"Thursday after the arcade closes. Larsen thought we ought to get together before Connan returns from New York."

Alicia's pulse gave an undisciplined leap at the mention of his name, but she stoically ignored it. "I'll be there. I'm going to tell them about my decision and give them an idea of what's available in Portland. I'm going to tell them that I think that Connan is right. The arcade is a dead end, and I think everyone would be better off someplace else."

Ignoring Martha's exasperated expression, she lifted her chin, squared her shoulders and marched back to the Pantry.

Richard pounced on her the minute she walked through the door and dragged her over to the freezer to look at his dolphin. She dutifully admired the lumpy block of ice, although as far as she could tell it didn't look much like a dolphin or anything else.

"It's just beginning to take shape," he explained. "This is the head and the arching back and the tail, of course. I'll start the chisel work this afternoon after it hardens up a bit. I can only keep it out of the freezer for forty minutes at a time."

"I'll be anxious to see the finished product," she said with a forced note of enthusiasm.

* * *

On Wednesday Alicia pursued real estate doggedly. As she crossed addresses off her list, she began to wonder if the agent had given her his dead-duck file. Nothing came even close to what she needed.

By three o'clock she had looked at all but two of the sites on her list, and it was almost time to head home. She still had to shower and change before driving out to Pheasant Run. Richard would need her help pulling together the last-minute details for the bank party.

She glanced at the addresses again and decided to at least drive by. They couldn't possibly be any worse than what she'd already looked at. She turned a corner and found herself in a well-kept neighborhood business district three blocks long. There was a movie theater on the corner, as well as a bookstore, and a record shop and a grocery store. She slowed as she looked for the address, conscious of the faint excitement rising in her.

The area was perfect, the businesses all looked prosperous, and there was a dense residential district surrounding them. Pulling over to the curb, she parked Mable and climbed down. There it was, sandwiched between a spotless butcher's shop and a florist. Peering through the window, she knew that she had found what she had been looking for. The space was easily double what she had at the arcade. Her mind clicked into gear, and she began to furnish and equip the space in her imagination. If lease terms were acceptable, her search had ended.

Looking at her watch, she turned reluctantly back toward Mable. She had to get going. She'd call the agent in the morning and arrange to get inside. Richard would have to look at it as well, and then she could begin to work on the legal and financial details. She gripped Mable's steering wheel for a moment and let relief and triumph wash over her.

Chapter Nine

The ice dolphin was a tremendous hit with the bank personnel, and the food seemed to vanish almost as soon as it was placed on the table. Alicia had left a stack of business cards in a discreet corner, and they had disappeared with flattering speed. As she chatted with the guests about the food and the ice carving, several individuals approached her about parties they were planning. For the Pantry the evening was a triumph, but Alicia was withdrawn and preoccupied.

She should have been able to take more pleasure in the evening's resounding success. Her hard work and talent had paid off, and she deserved to savor her accomplishments. But there was no chance of that while thoughts of Connan O'Rourke occupied so much of her mind. The shadow he cast eclipsed the bright, congratulatory faces that surrounded her. It was one more black mark on a long grudge list as far as she was concerned. If any further evidence of his domineering personality had been needed, she had it now.

He had been gone for five days, but his influence had not faded at all. She had thought it would be a relief not to have to deal with his physical presence, but she had discovered his presence in her mind was even more disconcerting. Unwillingly she found herself wishing that he had heard the compliments and witnessed the respect she received from these high-powered businesspeople. He would have had to admit that she had talents other than the obvious ones that he admired.

She fought against admitting it, but she wanted Connan. He had made her say the words, and she had complied because they were the truth. For her, the wanting had been a part of love and respect and for a short, bright moment she had assumed that it had been the same for him. Thank God his domineering attitude had shattered the illusion before she had a chance to betray how naïve she really was.

The party's over, she thought as her eyes passed over the rapidly dwindling crowd.

Thursday morning Alicia dropped by Larsen's jewelry shop, intending to discuss her new perspective on the arcade. At her tentative disclosure that she had been looking at retail locations in Portland, he exploded into a fiery monologue and ended by reassuring her that the tenants were all behind her and wouldn't allow her to be forced out.

She listened impatiently for ten minutes, occasionally trying to insert a few comments, but Larsen wasn't listening. She had the distinct impression that he was practicing his speech for the afternoon's meeting. Unwilling to hear it twice, she excused herself and walked toward the Pantry. If Larsen was a reliable barometer of the tenants' temper, she had better conserve her own energy for the coming confrontation. She had the uncomfortable suspicion she was going to need all the strength she could muster.

Alicia found herself counting the hours to the meeting with a mixture of impatience and dread. She wanted to get the unpleasant business over with so that she could put the arcade and Connan behind her and focus on her relocation. Once she got things sorted out, she would be free once and for all of the painful memories and persistent yearnings that plagued her.

"Damn the man," she muttered furiously. She didn't know what upset her the most—Connan's persistent pursuit or her own susceptibility to his intense masculinity.

At three she promptly sent Richard home and locked the shop doors. Then she prowled restlessly around the kitchen until it was time to join the others at Martha's establishment.

Someone had set up folding chairs in a neat semicircle near the rockers in the corner where Martha was holding court. They all looked up when Alicia walked in. "Here's the woman of the hour now," joked Ben, owner of the bookstore.

Alicia cringed and answered coolly, "Hardly that, I think."

She sat down in the empty rocker next to Martha and took a deep breath. Martha gave her a wink and cleared her throat before speaking, drawing everyone's attention. "We wanted to get together today to talk about our future in the arcade." A babble of angry voices prevented her from going any farther. Alicia closed her eyes in despair. The next half hour was a nightmare of complaints and invective as the tenants aired real and imagined grievances against Connan. She tried to inject a note of balance by challenging some of the more outrageous charges, but she was shouted down.

"I hope you're enjoying this," she hissed in Martha's ear.

Martha smiled angelically and nodded in satisfaction. "It's better than I hoped for."

Alicia scowled at her and decided that she had heard enough. She stood up abruptly and yelled as loudly as she could, "Be quiet."

Half a dozen pairs of startled eyes focused on her flushed face. "Thank you for your kind attention," she said sweetly. "I have something to say to you all."

She paused and drew a deep breath. She had to make it good because this would be her only chance to turn the tide. Her own conscience and the welfare of these people who were her friends and associates depended on it.

"When I first learned about Mr. O'Rourke's plan to phase out the arcade, I was angry. I'd worked hard in my shop, as we all have, and the thought of being forced out made me furious. My immediate response was to fight back."

There were growls of agreement from her audience, and Alicia heard Larsen mutter, "Damn right."

"So I talked it over with Martha, and we decided to try and organize all the tenants to resist the phase-out." Light applause rippled throughout the room, and Alicia gritted her teeth.

"I was so busy reacting that I didn't take the time to do any thinking. I'm afraid that redheads have a reputation for that kind of thing." Everyone laughed and relaxed in their chairs.

"When the dust began to settle, I realized that I hadn't really listened to any of Mr. O'Rourke's well-thought-out reasons for closing the arcade. The more I thought about it, the more I recognized the validity of his arguments. I started to do some comparison shopping and I realized he was right."

The tenants shifted in their chairs and began to rustle papers. Alicia knew she was losing them. She rushed to finish what she had to say.

"The arcade is too isolated, and the available space is too limited to make for a viable retail center. I've looked at a lot of property over the past few days and I've found a perfect location for the Pantry in Portland. I know that all of you could do the same. The arcade is a dead end."

Angry voices rose and surrounded her as she sank back down into the rocking chair beside Martha. She hunched her shoulders in defeat. She hadn't managed to convince them of the mistake they were making.

Ben, the owner of the bookstore, stood up and faced Alicia. "I think we can all understand if you don't feel up to fighting what could be a messy battle. I want you to know that we don't hold it against you."

Alicia's eyes narrowed in disbelief. They thought she was backing down because she was afraid. They hadn't heard a word of what she had said.

Ben swaggered a little and threw out his chest. "I believe that I can speak for everyone when I say that we're not going to let anyone push us around." He looked around at the grimly nodding faces for confirmation and smiled with satisfaction. "And despite the fact that Alicia won't be with us in the trenches, I think she deserves a big hand for bringing this intolerable situation to our attention. Without her information, we might have been too late to fight it." To her intense mortification they all stood up and subjected her to a hearty round of applause. It was worse than anything she had expected, and she turned to Martha for support, but Martha's face wore an expression of stunned horror as she gazed at the doorway. Alicia turned reluctantly in the same direction, knowing with deadly intuition whom she would find there.

Connan's tall, broad-shouldered frame filled the doorway, and Alicia could see his face quite clearly above the heads of the others. His expression had a hard edge to it, and his flinty eyes bored into her with unalloyed contempt. She felt herself begin to wither under that look.

He obviously had only heard the last few minutes of the meeting and wasn't aware that she had tried to support his plans for the arcade. He was looking at her as if she was a particularly nasty specimen of humanity, a traitorous, sneaking excuse for a person.

Alicia was sickened by what she read in his eyes. She had been able to handle his passion, his attempts at domination, even his anger, but his scathing condemnation she found strangely wounding.

Her knuckles went white as she gripped the arms of the rocking chair and fought down the impulse to explain the scene he had just witnessed. She didn't owe him anything, she told herself fiercely, and if he wanted to think the worst of her, that was fine with her. At least if he was disgusted by her, he wouldn't bother her anymore. The thought was followed by a prickling of tears behind her eyes. She turned her face from him and gazed stonily at her hands.

Connan stepped confidently into the shop before anyone else was aware of his presence and spoke easily. "Is this a private party, or can anyone join in?"

The shop owners moved together, as if closing ranks, and looked embarrassed. Ben spoke belligerently into the awkward silence. "We've found out about your plans for the arcade, O'Rourke, and we don't like it."

Connan interrupted smoothly and sympathetically. "I don't blame you a bit. It's disconcerting to get important information secondhand. I'm sorry it came out this way and upset you all. I had planned on getting together with everyone next week, but since you're all here now, why don't you come up to my office and get comfortable. I know we can work this out to everyone's satisfaction."

They're almost eating out of his hand, Alicia thought with detached admiration. He had diffused the charged atmosphere in a matter of minutes with his easy charm and convincing concern. With a few words, he had reduced the situation to a mere misunderstanding, and the previously hostile group was following him out of Martha's cramped shop as if he were the Pied Piper.

"Now, that's what I call a surprise," Martha said, breaking the uneasy silence.

"Was it really, Martha? Do you mean that you didn't call Connan and let him know about our little meeting? It certainly added an interesting twist to the proceedings."

"I guess I deserved that, but no, Alicia, I didn't say a word to Connan. It's just an unfortunate coincidence."

"It's not important," Alicia said dully. "It was only a matter of time before he found out anyway."

Martha looked at her thoughtfully. "Yes, well, it's too bad that he thinks you're the villain in this soap opera, especially after the way you stood up for him."

Alicia straightened her back. "I don't care what he thinks, and I wouldn't waste my time standing up for him. I was only pointing out that his reasons for shutting down the arcade were logical and made sense to me."

"Get off your soapbox, Red. I believe you. I'd be the last person to accuse you of any personal involvement. Some folks might think you've gotten awfully cozy with Connan, but not me." Martha looked at her with a provoking glint in her eye.

"Personal involvement?" Alicia almost shrieked, and Martha settled placidly into her chair and began to rock.

"You're a devil, Martha Trotter, and I'm leaving before I'm tempted to strangle you." Alicia jumped up and stalked out of the shop without another word.

As she walked back to the Pantry, the sounds of Martha's hoarse chuckles followed her. The woman's blatant insinuations infuriated her. Did the tenants really think she had changed her position on the arcade because of a personal involvement with Connan O'Rourke?

She felt like slamming doors and breaking windows. The man tainted everything he came into contact with. It hadn't been easy standing up in front of her friends and admitting that she had been wrong.

Now that little act of courage was being twisted into something reprehensible, and it was all his fault. Connan O'Rourke was a spoiler, she thought bitterly, and if she wanted to salvage anything she had better move quickly.

Checking the time, she quickly dialed the real estate office and gave a sigh of relief when Ted answered the phone.

"Ted, I'm glad I caught you. I've found a shop that I'd like to look at. Would it be possible for me to get a key and see it tonight?"

He was eager to be helpful and assured her that he never left the office until six-thirty anyway. She had plenty of time to drive back to Portland and pick up the key.

Alicia locked up in record time and headed for the parking lot. As she climbed into Mable, her eyes strayed to the top-floor windows of Connan's office. The lights were on, and she assumed he was busy charming everyone. Recognizing the wistful trend of her thoughts, she shoved them to the back of her mind and turned the van down the drive.

The autumn twilight came early and gave the countryside a familiar, intimate look. Alicia knew that she would miss the daily drives out of the bustling city into this quiet, pastoral beauty. On the other hand, she reminded herself, commuting wasted a lot of time—time she would be able to invest in her business.

Her thoughts seesawed back and forth. She would miss the tranquil days at Pheasant Run but would enjoy the excitement and challenge of the city. She would miss Martha's acerbic companionship, but she would be freed of Connan O'Rourke's domineering intrusions. Once she moved, she'd never have to see him again.

A sound suspiciously like a sob came out of her throat. She kept the tears at bay with sheer willpower, but the thoughts that had inspired them tumbled unrestrainedly through her mind.

She picked up the key at Ted's office and drove straight to the shop. She needed something concrete to look at, to think about, something to drive out the creeping regrets that were wrapping around her thoughts.

The shop was dark and looked a little forlorn in the row of prosperously active businesses. She unlocked the door and fumbled for a light switch. The single sixty-watt bulb did little to enhance the deserted space, but Alicia resolutely began to pace off the interior and make notes.

It looked as if there would be room for about ten tables as well as a larger display case. The room would easily accommodate double the shelving that she had at the arcade. She would definitely be able to carry a larger range of regional products as well as expand her selection of imports.

She walked back into the kitchen area and looked at the layout with approval. It was roomy with lots of counter space. Three or four people would be able to work together without getting trampled. However, most of the equipment was in bad shape. She'd have to get Richard to check it out before she made an offer.

Reluctantly she turned off the lights and locked the door. She didn't feel like going back to her empty apartment, but she couldn't do anything more in the deserted shop. The next step would be to get Richard to look it over, then talk to Ted about terms.

She stood on the sidewalk and looked down the block. With surprise, she realized that it was almost deserted. She checked her watch and saw that it was after ten.

She walked back to the van and headed for home. She felt emotionally exhausted but doubted that sleep would come easily to her that night. There was too much on her mind. She tried to shrug off the unwanted melancholy, telling herself that she was wasting too much time in bolstering her flagging spirits.

It was O'Rourke's fault, she thought with a little flare of anger. He was so alive, so compelling, that anything that didn't include him seemed colorless by comparison. "Like my life," she whispered bleakly.

She finally admitted the loss she felt, the grief of not having his stormy, vital presence in her life. He had excited her one moment and infuriated her the next, but every time they had been together she had felt gloriously alive.

Automatically Alicia steered the van into the parking garage of her apartment building. She opened the door, jumped lightly to the ground and made her way toward the elevators. She pushed the button and slumped against the wall to wait.

Suddenly a tall shape moved from the shadows, and a large muscular hand wrapped around her arm. "Where the hell have you been?"

Alicia swallowed the startled scream that had been on her lips and tilted her head back to look into Connan's eyes. The overhead fluorescent lighting made him look unnaturally pale and gave his narrowed eyes a silvery gleam. He looked slightly rumpled, she thought, and wondered if the tenants had been harder to handle than he had anticipated.

"I've been waiting for you for three hours," he growled at her, and gave her arm a little shake. "Where have you been?"

Alicia's temper began to smolder. They'd been together for only a minute and he was already pushing her. Her instinctive pleasure at seeing him was beginning to fade. She looked pointedly at his hand on her arm and then back at his grim face. "You're hurting me."

His fingers loosened immediately, but he didn't release her. "I've been worried," he said. He looked at her hungrily, without a trace of the chilling contempt she had read in his eyes earlier. His arm slid around her waist, and he pulled her against his body, holding her close.

Alicia felt a familiar heat rise in her body, overwhelming her with a tide of longing. Her hands curled around his neck as her lips parted beneath his insistent mouth. The hot stroking of his tongue across her trembling lips sent ripples of aching sensation through her body, and when his hand cupped the swollen fullness of her breast, she almost cried out from the piercing sweetness of the caress.

Without will or reason, she simply responded with all the untapped passion of her being to the man she loved.

Dimly she became aware that Connan had muttered something against her lips and was turning away from her. As she struggled out of the sensual haze, she wanted to protest, to tell him that she didn't want him to go. Then she realized he had her hand in a hard grip and was pulling her away from the elevator.

"Wait—what...?" she whispered in total confusion.

Connan looked down at her with a trace of impatience. "I said I can't take it anymore. We're going to my house."

Alicia stood very still as the last of the glowing warmth faded and a chill started up her spine. He had done it again. He weakened her will with his drugging kisses and then started telling her what to do. He never asked; he just gave orders and expected her to fall in line. What could love mean to a man like him? Probably nothing at all, she thought bitterly.

The love she couldn't help feeling for him was all mixed up with pain and anger and resentment. Why couldn't he love her for what she was? How could he be so tender and caring one moment and then order her around like a half-witted servant the next? Dear God, why had he made her love him?

Something snapped inside her, and suddenly the sound of all her pain and frustration came pouring out. She hurled the words at him as she beat blindly at his chest with small fists.

"Damn you, Connan O'Rourke. You're just like Peter. Everything has to go your way. You never ask, you just take and take until there's nothing left. Well, you're not going to do that to me. I won't let you."

He didn't say anything. He just looked at her with darkened eyes and pulled her tightly against his body. One large brown hand captured her two smaller ones and held them against his chest. Alicia could feel the relentless pounding of his heart beneath her palms, and she gave a little shiver of fear.

Connan felt as if he were poised on the brink of the hell she had consigned him to. If he made one false step, he knew he would lose her forever. She hadn't been able to hide how wounded she was, how much he had hurt her. His arms tightened fractionally. God, all he wanted to do was kiss away that bruised look around her eyes and tell her how much he loved her. It took every ounce of his formidable willpower to resist doing just that. It would only drive her farther away from him. All the mistakes and misunderstandings had to be cleared away before they could finally come together.

With infinite tenderness, he cupped her chin and tilted her face so that he could see her eyes. "Alicia, I never meant to hurt you. Please believe me."

His voice was deep and soft, smoothing away the jagged edges of her pain. Alicia felt the tightly coiled muscles of her body begin to relax.

"Just let me talk to you. This time I'm asking. Please come back with me to the house. It's quiet there and we won't be disturbed. We can talk, and maybe we can finally put an end to all this hurting we both feel."

Alicia nodded with resignation. She was too exhausted to speak, too drained to fight him any longer. Yes, she thought dully, let's put an end to it once and for all.

She walked in the circle of his arm to his car and got in. Connan started the powerful engine of the Porsche, and without speaking, drove away from the lights of the city into the calm, quiet night toward Pheasant Run.

Chapter Ten

The Porsche turned smoothly between the two stone pillars that flanked the entrance to Pheasant Run and then angled off to the right on a narrow, winding road that led to the old caretaker's house. They drove through a small grove of trees, and when they emerged on the other side, Alicia could see an old stone house that was built on a low rise of land.

It was two stories high with a steeply pitched roof and a massive river-rock chimney against one end. The moon had risen, and by its clear light, Alicia could see bay windows and small diamond-shaped panes of glass.

Connan shut off the engine and quietly walked around the car to open her door. He held out a strong, capable hand to her and stood silently waiting in the black-and-silver moonlight. Alicia looked from him to the house and thought how alike they were—strong and enduring, a haven if you were inside the walls, a fortress if you were on the outside.

She put her hand in his and let him draw her toward the massive oak door. She didn't dare let hope loose in her heart again. She could only move hesitantly from minute to minute. By expecting nothing perhaps she could avoid the pain of disappointment.

Alicia was afraid to meet his eyes as they stopped in front of the door. She had betrayed too much of her tumultuous emotions already, and she didn't want him to read her final secret as well.

She looked around the paved stone entryway as Connan switched on a dim lamp and then followed him into the living room. It was a large room dominated by a huge stone fireplace at one end. The walls were plastered a soft white, and dark wooden beams were exposed in the ceiling.

Connan knelt on the hearth and set a match to the pile of kindling in the grate. He had tossed his jacket aside, and Alicia could see the powerful stretch of muscle beneath the fabric of his shirt. When he stood and turned, the firelight seemed to flicker in his eyes.

"Sit down, Alicia." He gestured toward a deep couch pulled up in front of the fireplace. "Would you like some cognac?"

"Yes, thank you," she replied stiltedly. It would give her something to do with her hands. Her eyes followed him as he crossed the room and opened a carved cabinet. His movements were awkward, and as she watched, he spilled some of the cognac on the polished wood. He mopped it up with a wad of napkins and cursed softly.

Alicia realized with astonishment that he was nervous. She looked at him curiously as he came toward her with the brandy snifters cradled in his hands. There was a hesitancy in his approach that she had never seen before.

He stopped in front of her, looking impossibly tall, but for once she didn't feel intimidated by the sheer size of him. He reached down and handed her the glass, warm from his hand, and she cupped it in both palms. He stood indecisively as she bent her head to breathe in the heady, aromatic fumes.

Connan raised his own glass to his lips and took a sip of the amber liquid. Then he sat down at the opposite end of the couch and said softly, "Tell me about Peter, Alicia. Tell me about the man who hurt you, the one who's been standing between us since the beginning."

The firelight picked out strands of gold in her fiery hair and turned the cognac in her glass into a pool of molten light. She took a sip and felt the liquor race through her body like a hot, surging flood. She stared at the flames for a long, silent moment, turning Connan's words over in her mind. She had thought that she had pushed Peter firmly into the past and shut the door. She had assumed he no longer had the power to influence her or cause any more pain.

Now Connan was telling her that Peter stood between them like some malevolent ghost, and perhaps he was right. Perhaps she had allowed those memories to fester within her, blinding her so completely that she couldn't even recognize truth when she saw it. Hesitantly she began speaking in a casual tone, as if the story she told had happened to someone else, someone she didn't know very well.

"I met Peter when I was twenty-one. I was working in a wine shop in Eugene, and he was a sales representative for a big California winery. He seemed very sophisticated, very exciting, compared to my other dates. He was tall and dark and muscular—every girl's dream come true." The words tasted bitter in her mouth, and she took another sip of cognac.

"Of course, all of my so-called dates had been friends of my brothers, and they all treated me more like one of the gang, or maybe a little sister. I was very naive, and when Peter began to send me flowers and call me a week in advance for a date, I was overwhelmed by the attention. He made me feel like a woman, alluring and desirable, instead of the runt of the litter."

Connan watched the remembered pain scour her features and felt his own fists clench in response. He wanted to hold her, to kiss away all the ugly memories and give her ones of joy in their place. But he knew he had to control himself. Alicia needed to talk it all out, and he had to listen. He had no doubt that it would be a painful exorcism for both of them, but it was the only way to clear away the past and make room for the future.

"He traveled a lot for his job, but whenever he was home I spent every available minute of my time with him. He took an interest in everything I did. He signed me up for gourmet cooking classes so that I could prepare his favorite dishes. He suggested a different style of dressing—something more feminine, he said. He introduced me to new people who he said were more interesting and polished than my old friends."

Her voice wavered, and a glaze of tears made the fire seem suddenly blurred. She pushed her hair back impatiently and lifted her chin before continuing defiantly.

"At first I was so glad to see him whenever he returned from a business trip that I agreed eagerly to everything he suggested. After a while, though, he didn't suggest, he just made arrangements. I thought it was because he loved me, because he wanted to take care of me. Almost before I knew what had happened, he had isolated me from the rest of the world, from my friends, from my family. As far as he was concerned, the only thing worthy of my attention was him, and nothing else was allowed to compete."

"My God, Alicia. Couldn't your family see what was happening? What about those brothers of yours?" Connan's fury broke through his self-imposed silence. "You were slowly being smothered to death."

Alicia turned her gaze from the fire and looked at Connan's fierce expression. The suppressed violence she saw there made her smile faintly, and she felt vaguely comforted at his anger on her behalf. Her smile turned bitter again as she considered his question.

"The boys tried to talk to me, but at first I wouldn't listen. I thought it was just more of the big-brother bullying that they had dished out all the time I was growing up. Later I was too proud to admit that they had been right."

She forced her eyes to turn away from his intent expression. She couldn't look at him while she finished her sordid little story; she couldn't bear to see his compassion turn to disgust.

"I was alone and desperate. Peter had done such a thorough job of undermining my self-confidence that I believed our deteriorating relationship was my fault. He spent more and more time away on business trips, and when we were together, he became increasingly critical of everything I did. No matter how hard I tried, I couldn't satisfy him.''

She took a fortifying sip of cognac, but this time the mellow heat didn't come close to melting the ice in her veins. Her voice was like a brittle thread that threatened to snap.

''The accusations you made the night of the wine tasting struck rather close to home. You accused me of trying to sell myself.'' Her laugh grated unpleasantly in the firelit room. ''You were wrong that night, but I guess you could say that I tried it once and couldn't interest the buyer....''

''Stop it, Alicia.'' Connan's voice cut like the edge of a blade across the space between them. Then, unable to listen to her scathing self-contempt, he was at her side and wrapping his arms around her shuddering body.

''I didn't mean a word of that, Alicia. It was anger and frustration talking. God, what a fool I've been. No wonder you looked as if you hated me.''

Alicia let her cheek soak up the warmth of his chest, but she still couldn't meet his eyes. She had to tell him the rest of it. She didn't want there to be any secrets between them.

''We hadn't slept together.'' Her voice trembled as she continued. ''I wanted to wait until we got married. Peter used to tease me about being a virgin, but toward the end it became more of a taunt.''

Connan's hand was stroking her hair with a gentle, smoothing motion. She could feel the rise and fall of his chest against her cheek, and she breathed in his musky, masculine scent. Somehow his closeness gave her the courage to go on.

"It was a Friday, and I was waiting at my apartment for him. He had been away on business for two weeks and our parting had been an angry one—he had been angry with me. I had cooked his favorite meal and bought his favorite wine, and I had decided that I would let him make love to me.

"I was incredibly naive, and I thought that my capitulation would make everything all right again and we would live happily ever after. Well, he was late and the dinner was ruined, and when I told him what I had decided he laughed at me. He said that he had plenty of better offers and that he was bored with playing patty-cake. Then he left."

Connan shifted and pulled her onto his lap. His arms folded even more securely around her as he lowered his head and covered her lips with a gentle exploratory kiss. Alicia felt a trickle of warmth in her veins, and she raised her hands to the strong column of his throat. Beneath her fingers she could feel the hard beat of his pulse under the taut skin.

She felt the fear and all the old humiliation wash away as the overwhelming tides of longing swept over her. She pressed herself more intimately against Connan's body, as if she could absorb some of his strength by the closer contact.

"I swore that I'd never let anyone take over my life that way again. I was bitterly humiliated at my own slavishness, and I promised myself success and independence in the future. I created Panache Pantry and poured every ounce of myself into making it successful."

Connan turned his face into the thick mass of curls that lay against her neck. "And then I came along, axing the symbol of your independence and pursuing you with all the finesse of a one-man SWAT team. My God, no wonder you couldn't stand the sight of me."

"I was afraid," she said slowly as a confusing swirl of images slowed and coalesced. "All this time I've been afraid of getting involved with another Peter—a taker, a spoiler."

She pushed away from him so she could see his lucid gray eyes. "But I've just realized that the thing I was truly afraid of was that I had nothing left to give."

She finished on a note of wonder, amazed at how she had been able to deceive herself for so long. She had been suffering from an outsized inferiority complex all this time, she thought indignantly.

Connan saw the returning flash in her brilliant eyes with relief. As he had come to expect, her indomitable spirit refused to stay down for long. His eyes were drawn irresistibly to her soft poppy-colored lips, and the too familiar ache of desire spread deep in his stomach. He bent his head to hers.

"I love you, Alicia." His words vibrated against her lips with a delicious friction, and it took her a moment to absorb his meaning. Then the syllables danced unrestrainedly in her heart, and she laughed with relief at the honest intensity in his voice.

"No, you don't," she retorted, determined to get all the troublesome details out in the open. "You're disgusted with me for being underhanded about the arcade, and you can't stand virgins."

His chest rumbled with silent, contained laughter as his lips traveled the delicate sweep of her jaw and came to rest at her throat.

"Don't contradict me, you excruciating redhead. I love you and all your fiery independence and strength. I'm glad," he continued fiercely, "I'm glad you've never belonged to anyone else. Since knowing you, I've discovered I'm a jealous brute at heart." He tilted her head up so he could look into her clear green eyes.

"I know I've made a lot of stupid mistakes, Alicia. But believe me, I never meant to hurt you. I was so caught up in my own hunger that I didn't stop to consider that you might feel differently, that you might have other needs. I was in love for the first time in my life, and it never occurred to me that the feeling might not be reciprocated."

"You were arrogant," Alicia murmured.

"Yes, I suppose I was arrogant...."

"And bossy." Her words came out a little shakily.

"Bossy?" He was indignant and then suspicious. Capturing her chin, he made her meet his eyes again and saw the mischief veiled behind her lowered lashes.

He settled back against the cushions and began to speak in an impersonal, analytical voice. "Of course, you were maddening, obstructive and uncooperative. Then there's your awful temper—"

"You can stop right there, O'Rourke, or I'll give you a taste of temper." Alicia struggled ineffectually to put some distance between them.

"And that's another thing," he continued as if he hadn't heard her interruption. "I won't have you calling me O'Rourke once we're married."

Alicia's struggles subsided, and she turned to look wonderingly at his face. There were no grim lines around his mouth, no trace of harshness in his broad forehead, and from his eyes there beamed an unmistakable message of love. At that moment she closed the door once and for all on the bitter memories of the past and turned her face to the future.

"Are you telling or asking me, Connan?" She couldn't resist the impulse to tease him.

He looked at her sharply and then relaxed when he saw the familiar dancing lights in her eyes. "Well," he drawled, "I guess I'm asking you to marry me and telling you that I'm going to marry you."

Laughter bubbled out of her throat like a spring. "I love you, Connan O'Rourke."

"It's about time," he said huskily as his hands began to familiarize themselves with the graceful dips and swells of her body.

Epilogue

Alicia scanned the crowded room with lingering satisfaction. The new Panache Pantry would be a smashing success if the size of the opening-party crowd was anything to go by. The lavish assortment of appetizers was gobbled up almost as soon as the trays hit the table. And the amount of champagne they consumed...

Purposefully she made her way toward Connan's broad shoulders on the opposite side of the room. She slipped her hand into the crook of his arm and began to massage it urgently. He gave her a look that made her tingle and excused himself to the real estate developer he had been talking with.

"If you don't stop that, sweetheart, you're going to miss the rest of your party."

She pressed herself lightly against his arm and then pulled herself away. "Connan, they've drunk all the champagne."

He smiled down at her and tucked her hand back into his arm. "What did you expect, love? After all, it is from Pheasant Run."

"Yes, but the opening is supposed to last for another forty-five minutes, and there's nothing left for this horde to drink."

"Well, I gave Richard an extra case to break out for the staff when this was over. I suppose you could give that to your future clients and the staff could make do with cognac."

"Have I told you how much I love you, how much your encouragement has meant to me through all this?"

"Not recently," he growled. "And I can't say I approve of your timing."

"I'll make it up to you later," she promised. "I have a surprise for you." Deftly she eluded his restraining hands and slipped through the crowd, tossing him a mischievous glance over her shoulder.

Later, as they sat in front of the old stone fireplace, Alicia tipped her head back against Connan's shoulder. "Aren't you curious about my secret?"

"Yes, but I refuse to satisfy your penchant for teasing me by asking any questions."

She raised her hand to his chest and began to toy with the buttons on his shirt. "It's been a busy six months, hasn't it? I'd forgotten how time-consuming it is to open a business." She looked at him from under her lashes and added, "Of course, this time I had a few other things on my mind as well."

"I should hope so," he said as he captured her hand and began nibbling kisses against the soft pads of her fingertips. "Marrying me, and moving all that delightful lingerie into my bedroom, taking over my closets, criticizing the condition of my kitchen.'' His voice lowered huskily as one hand slid to tease her breast. "Loving me."

"Yes," she agreed breathlessly as his thumb began to circle slowly against her softness. Her thoughts were scattering before his purposeful seduction, and she blurted out, "I've decided to take a partner."

"You've already got a partner, and the idea of a triumvirate doesn't appeal to me."

"Connan, be serious. I'm talking about the Pantry. I want to make Richard a partner."

Her words finally captured his attention, but she found herself regretting his suddenly stilled hands.

"Why do you want to do that?" he asked quietly.

She raised a finger to lovingly trace the clean line of his upper lip. "I guess I'm greedy," she said. "I want to spend more time with you. I resent the thought of having to chase off to some godforsaken wedding reception with a tray of stuffed mushrooms when I could be spending the time with you."

Connan looked chagrined. "Did I really say that? It must have been under extreme provocation.... Seriously, though, I knew that I was marrying the Pantry as well when I married you. I'd never ask you to give it up."

"I don't want to give it up," she admitted. "But I thought if I made Richard a partner, with the understanding that he take over the actual catering part of things, then our schedules would be more compatible. I would be involved with the planning and the day-to-day operation of the deli, and he would take care of the night and weekend stuff. What do you think?"

"I think it's a marvelous idea. I've been feeling a little neglected lately... all those long hours you've been putting in getting ready for the opening." He paused, and Alicia recognized the signs that he was about to say something outrageous. "All those lonely nights when you had a headache or were too tired..."

"I never have headaches," she sputtered indignantly, and then subsided when she realized she had risen to his bait. "In fact, you may be the one with the headaches now that I have all that unaccustomed time to fill up."

"I suppose you could always redesign the kitchen if you've nothing better to do," he suggested blandly.

Alicia's eyes lit up at the idea. Connan's expert renovations of the lovely old stone house had not been extended to the kitchen. It was large and sunny and languishing under innumerable coats of chipped pink enamel.

"That would keep me interested for a while," she agreed. "Do you have any other little projects in mind?"

"There's the rest of the remodeling, the sun porch, the greenhouse, the gardens."

"Sounds like fun." Alicia didn't trust his innocent smile for a minute.

"And, of course, there's the upstairs."

"Of course," she echoed agreeably.

"And then there's the redheaded dynasty I've always wanted to found...."

"Dynasty?" Alicia's voice wobbled as the image of Connan's baby in her arms flooded her with warmth.

"Don't you want children? You know the only way I was able to get Martha to vacate the arcade was by bribing her with the promise of lots of babies to knit things for."

"Martha . . . lots of babies?" Alicia sputtered helplessly. He had done it again—turned her upside down with his disreputable sense of humor.

"But, darling, I promised." His voice was shamelessly imploring. "Besides, my dreams have been haunted by visions of a pack of redheaded hooligans, just like you and your brothers, overrunning the grounds of Pheasant Run."

"I was not a hooligan," she objected automatically. "I was a tomboy."

"Fine. Then we'll have four or five tomboys tearing up the grounds."

"Two," she said firmly. "A boy and a girl."

He lifted her high against his chest and started walking toward the bedroom. "I'll flip you for it," he said.

"Two out of three," she said, determined to have the last word.

COMING NEXT MONTH

LOGAN'S WOMAN—Glenda Sands
Susan belonged to another man—or so Clark Haggerty thought. And
it was up to Susan to reinforce that belief. But that was easier said
than done once she found herself falling in love with him.

TOMORROW'S DAWN—Frances Lloyd
Justine Carroll had once loved Marcus Glendinning, but he had
married another woman. Now he had returned, determined to win her
back. Did he deserve another chance?

LADY AND THE LEGEND—Sharon De Vita
Victoria Fairchild was a lady—even though she wasn't acting like one.
It couldn't have anything to do with Gator McCallister—could it?

BENEATH A SUMMER MOON—Juli Greene
Raising two sons and running a garden center kept widow
Janice Haley busy, but she longed for a man to make her feel like a woman
again. Why did that man have to be the impossible David Phillips?

KISSING GAMES—Pamela Toth
Supernerd or Superman? When Patricia MacGregor first saw
Brad McKinney, she almost died. This was her dream date? Oh, no!
Then Brad set out to remind her that Clark Kent was only a
disguise—what was underneath was the real thing.

STRANGE ENCHANTMENT—Annette Broadrick
One enchanted evening, teacher Elizabeth Bannister saw ad executive
Dan Morgan across a crowded room. Mesmerized, both of them
knew that their lives would never be the same again.

AVAILABLE THIS MONTH:

SATIN AND WHITE LACE
Barbara Turner

DARE TO DREAM
Cara Colter

THE PROPER MISS PORTER
Ruth Langan

PURSUED BY LOVE
Caty Lear

SUGAR AND SPICE
Debbie Macomber

THE PRIVATE GARDEN
Arlene James

ATTRACTIVE, SPACE SAVING BOOK RACK

Display your most prized novels on this handsome and sturdy book rack. The hand-rubbed walnut finish will blend into your library decor with quiet elegance, providing a practical organizer for your favorite hard-or softcovered books.

Only $9.95

Approximately 16" x 8" when assembled

Assembles in seconds!

To order, rush your name, address and zip code, along with a check or money order for $10.70* ($9.95 plus 75¢ postage and handling) payable to *Silhouette Books*.

Silhouette Books
Book Rack Offer
901 Fuhrmann Blvd.
P.O. Box 1325
Buffalo, NY 14269-1325

Offer not available in Canada.

BKR-2R

*New York residents add appropriate sales tax.

**Breathtaking adventure and romance
in the mystical land of the pharaohs...**

YESTERDAY
~AND~
TOMORROW

ERIN YORKE

A young British archeologist, Cassandra Baratowa, embarks
on an adventurous romp through Egypt in search of Queen
Nefertiti's tomb—and discovers the love of her life!

Available in MARCH, or reserve your copy for February shipping by sending your
name, address, zip or postal code along with a check or money order for $4.70 (in-
cludes 75¢ for postage and handling) payable to Worldwide Library to:

In the U.S.	In Canada
Worldwide Library	Worldwide Library
901 Fuhrmann Blvd.	P.O. Box 609
Box 1325	Fort Erie, Ontario
Buffalo, NY 14269-1325	L2A 9Z9

Please specify book title with your order.

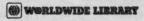 **WORLDWIDE LIBRARY**   YES-1

Take 4
Silhouette Special Edition novels
FREE...

and preview
future
books
in your
home for
15 days!

Start with 4 FREE books, yours to keep. Then, preview 6 brand-new Special Edition® novels—delivered right to your door every month—as soon as they are published.

When you decide to keep them, pay just $1.95 each ($2.50 each in Canada), *with no shipping, handling, or other additional charges of any kind!*

Romance *is* alive, well and flourishing in the moving love stories presented by Silhouette Special Edition. They'll awaken your desires, enliven your senses, and leave you tingling all over with excitement. In each romance-filled story you'll live and breathe the emotions of love and the satisfaction of romance triumphant.

You won't want to miss a single one of the heart-felt stories presented by Silhouette Special Edition; and when you take advantage of this special offer, you won't have to.

You'll also receive a FREE subscription to the Silhouette Books Newsletter as long as you remain a member. Each lively issue is filled with news on upcoming titles, interviews with your favorite authors, even their favorite recipes.

To become a home subscriber and receive your first 4 books FREE, fill out and mail the coupon today!

Silhouette Special Edition®

Silhouette Books, 120 Brighton Rd., P.O. Box 5084, Clifton, NJ 07015-5084

Clip and mail to: Silhouette Books, 120 Brighton Road, P.O. Box 5084, Clifton, NJ 07015-5084*

YES. Please send me 4 FREE Silhouette Special Edition novels. Unless you hear from me after I receive them, send me 6 new Silhouette Special Edition novels to preview each month. I understand you will bill me just $1.95 each, a total of $11.70 (in Canada, $2.50 each, a total of $15.00), with no shipping, handling, or other charges of any kind. There is no minimum number of books that I must buy, and I can cancel at any time. The first 4 books are mine to keep.   82SS87

Name	(please print)
Address	Apt. #
City State/Prov.	Zip/Postal Code

* In Canada, mail to: Silhouette Canadian Book Club, 320 Steelcase Rd., E., Markham, Ontario, L3R 2M1, Canada

Terms and prices subject to change.

SILHOUETTE SPECIAL EDITION is a service mark and registered trademark.   SE-SUB-2A

FOUR UNIQUE SERIES FOR EVERY WOMAN YOU ARE..

Silhouette Romance

Heartwarming romances that will make you laugh and cry as they bring you all the wonder and magic of falling in love.

6 titles per month

Silhouette Special Edition

Expanded romances written with emotion and heightened romantic tension to ensure powerful stories. A rare blend of passion and dramatic realism.

6 titles per month

Silhouette Desire

Believable, sensuous, compelling—and above all, romantic—these stories deliver the promise of love, the guarantee of satisfaction.

6 titles per month

Silhouette Intimate Moments

Love stories that entice; longer, more sensuous romances filled with adventure, suspense, glamour and melodrama.

4 titles per month

Silhouette Romances
not available in retail outlets in Canada

SIL-GEN-1A